Summer Road Trip

The Rapids

BY MELANIE DOWEIKO

EPIC Escape

An Imprint of EPIC Press
abdopublishing.com

The Rapids
Summer Road Trip

Written by Melanie Doweiko

Copyright © 2018 by Abdo Consulting Group, Inc.

Published by EPIC Press™
PO Box 398166
Minneapolis, MN 55439

All rights reserved.

Printed in the United States of America.

International copyrights reserved in all countries.
No part of this book may be reproduced in any form without
written permission from the publisher. EPIC Press™ is trademark
and logo of Abdo Consulting Group, Inc.

Cover design by Christina Doffing
Images for cover art obtained from iStock
Edited by Rue Moran

LIBRARY OF CONGRESS CATALOGING-IN-PUBLICATION DATA
Names: Doweiko, Melanie, author.
Title: The rapids/ by Melanie Doweiko
Description: Minneapolis, MN : EPIC Press, 2018 | Series: Summer road trip
Summary: Fourteen-year-old foster kid Tamika finds herself on the edge of the Missouri river
    in the grips of depression. However, events take a drastic turn when a stray rock and some
    quick thinking puts her in the company of a young couple on a source-to-sea kayaking trip
    down the river. Tamika begins to enjoy herself and becomes friends with the couple, but
    dark thoughts keep trying to creep in.
Identifiers: LCCN 2016962615 | ISBN 9781680767230 (lib. bdg.)
    | ISBN 9781680767797 (ebook)
Subjects: LCSH: Adventure stories—Fiction. | Travel—Fiction.
    | Depression in children—Fiction. | Runaway teenagers—Fiction | Young adult fiction.
Classification: DDC [FIC]—dc23
LC record available at http://lccn.loc.gov/2016962615

For my dad, who found a billion "better" ways to tie two kayaks to the roof of a truck

Chapter One

TAMIKA FELT PATHETIC. ALL SHE HAD TO DO WAS let gravity take over. Simple. Easy. Quick. But her body fought her.

She couldn't just let herself fall into the river. Or jump into the river. Or get a running start and throw herself into the river. Some instinct forced her to stop, tearing her from gravity's grip.

She grumbled as she walked along the bank of the Missouri, trying to skip rocks on the water. Bismarck, North Dakota. Miles from her most recent foster family. She'd hitched a ride and hopped out when she'd seen the sign for the city. Something like this would be even more impossible to do with witnesses. She preferred to be on her own, anyway.

That's what she tried to tell herself.

Maybe if she could find a better spot, she could do with her body what she was doing with the rocks. Would she skip when she hit the water?

The rocks skipped more easily the longer Tamika walked. How long would it take them to find her? Maybe it would be like the movies: a big, dramatic scene where they came running for her at the last second.

"Don't do it, Tamika!" they would shout. "We love you Tamika!"

She doubted it. Her foster family had made it clear that she was more of an unwelcome houseguest than a daughter, but that was nothing new. Most foster families had treated her like that. The best experience she could hope for was awkwardness.

It was never like the movies. Not even the ones *with* bad parents. Not for her. She almost wished it was. At least it would be obvious that she was hurting. Maybe someone would have helped her, maybe she'd have had the courage to stand up for herself and feel justified doing so. Instead, she felt like nothing.

Maybe she needed to jump from a higher point. She stuffed a few more rocks into her pockets and climbed an outcropping by the side of the river. At the top, she looked down. Her stomach dropped and her head spun. She'd never been a fan of heights, so why did she think she'd be able to jump from up here?

Stupid.

Useless.

Pathetic.

She made a noise somewhere between a groan and a scream and threw a rock for each of her shortcomings. Tamika ran out of rocks before she reached the end of the list. As she caught her breath, she wished she could actually attach her shortcomings to the rocks and be rid of them, but they were stuck to her and always would be. She'd have to settle for throwing herself into the river.

Slowly, carefully, Tamika inched down the

outcropping and back onto the riverbank. She began to stuff her pockets with more rocks. Would she sink, like the rocks did? She had heard somewhere that bodies float, but a million daytime crime investigation shows had taught her that they turned up at the bottoms of rivers as well. She doubted her death would be interesting enough for even a mention on a show like that.

One more dead black kid, but—and this is a shocker, folks—this one didn't get shot! She drowned!

. . . hardly even daytime news.

Would the police be the first to find her body? Or some campers? Or some kind of animal? Would they tell her foster family? How would they react? Would they even care? Were they even looking for her?

Maybe a more slippery spot would help her into the water faster.

Tamika continued along the riverbank, skipping every kind of rock she could find as she went. Maybe the river would run out of rocks before she could convince her body to let her do what she had come for. Maybe then the water would be so filled with rocks that she wouldn't be able to. Either way, she was fighting a losing battle.

Loser.

She growled and threw a handful of rocks into the water as hard as she could. They plunked and sank without a single skip. It didn't make her feel better. It didn't make her feel anything. Tamika scooped another fistful of rocks off the riverbank and threw those in, as well, just to have something to do. They made a bigger splash.

More rocks.

Plunk! And then a few straggler *plunks* made by the rocks that had separated from the group in midair. Tamika was out of rocks again. She dropped to her knees and scooped up more handfuls, throwing them with all her strength into the river as soon as she took them from the ground. She couldn't stop herself. She didn't want to, but she couldn't even if she had. The only things that existed were her and the rocks and the *plunks* they made when they hit the water.

Until one missed the river entirely.

Chapter Two

"**O**w!"

The noise broke Tamika out of her trance. The last she'd checked, she was the only person out here, but that had definitely been a human voice. She looked for the source.

Not far from where she was standing and right in her line of fire, a couple were floating in a pair of kayaks. One was bent over, holding his nose. The Kayaks made a hollow sound when they bumped together as the second person attempted to get a closer look at him.

How had she not noticed them? The kayaks were

fluorescent orange! She should have seen them coming from miles away, but she had been too absorbed in herself and her rocks.

Nice going, Tamika.

You're such a screwup, Tamika.

It was like watching a scene in a movie. The couple were too far from her, the action too ridiculous to be something from her real life or something that she had caused.

As she stared, the second person looked up from her wounded partner. Long, curly hair trying to escape from a loose ponytail flipped over her shoulder as her eyes found Tamika.

"Hey!" she shouted. Tamika froze, suddenly pulled into the scene. She turned to look behind her. Maybe the actual main character was back there, ready with a catch phrase and an apologetic smile. No such person appeared. It was just Tamika, just reality, and she had just hurt someone. Maybe she should run away.

The woman spoke again before Tamika had a

chance to make a decision. "Just what were you aimin' at, kid?"

"Uuuuhhh . . . "

"Uh?" the woman repeated. She bent over to speak to her partner, but said it loud enough for Tamika to hear. "Is your name 'Uh'?"

The woman's partner gave her a look that Tamika couldn't see.

"Yeah, his name isn't 'Uh,'" the woman said, looking back up at Tamika with a smirk. "So I think you missed your target." She turned her kayak in the direction of the bank Tamika was standing on, her partner holding onto his face with one hand and the back of the woman's kayak with the other.

Tamika knew that if she was still on that bank by the time they got there, she was going to be in trouble. Several levels of trouble.

Run, Stupid! Now is the time to run!

But she didn't.

Instead, she stood on the bank of the river, staring as the woman paddled herself and her partner up to her, then continued to stare as the woman got out and dragged the kayaks onto the shore, and didn't stop staring as the woman pulled a medical kit out of her kayak and went to tend to her partner.

Stop staring, you creep.

She couldn't help it. She hadn't been able to help it back when her third-grade foster family's angry German shepherd had attacked her, nor when Emma Lovett, the richest girl in the eighth grade, had shouted racial slurs into Tamika's seventh-grade self's face. Freezing up was just one more broken thing about her. She didn't even have a working fight-or-flight mechanism, but at least this time was less terrifying.

Wasn't it?

Her body wasn't sure, so she continued to stare, frozen.

After a few minutes, the woman gave Tamika a curious look.

"You, uh, you *do* know I was just kidding, right kid?" she said, "Like, you're not in trouble or anything."

"Oh," Tamika said. She turned her gaze to her feet.

"Right . . . " The woman looked around as if trying to find someone to rescue her from the awkward tension. She must have sensed that Tamika would never be able to.

"Where are your parents?" she asked.

"My parents?" It always came back to that, didn't it? She couldn't even walk into a *library* without someone asking her that. Why? Didn't they realize it was a sore topic for her? And why did she need parents to get a library card, anyway?

"Uhhh . . . " She'd been silent for too long. If she told them the truth about why she was here, they might call the police, or send her back to her foster family, or lock her up in some padded room somewhere. That's what they did to people who wanted to kill themselves, right?

Lie.

"I . . . uhm . . . they died. On the river. Last year." Her eyes darted over to the kayaks for a second. They were fluorescent orange, waterproof bags and gear strapped onto the front and back of both with what looked like a mix of bungee cords and rope. The man holding a bloody cloth to his nose sat in the one, resting next to the now-empty tandem kayak the woman had climbed out of.

"In a kayaking accident," she added. The woman raised an eyebrow. Tamika might as well have said that her name was Rocky Fishman and she had come to dance the river jig. She had never been a convincing liar, but she couldn't stop now. She just had to hope these people were as gullible as adults in cartoons.

"Yeah . . . " Tamika looked down again. "I'm still real tore up about it. And I wanted to . . . to come and honor their memory." That's what people did when their parents died, right? She had heard the phrase in a lot of TV shows and figured it would work here. The man, who had just been reaching for one of the bags, turned to look at her.

"Oh, *honey*. I'm so sorry for your loss," the woman said. Tamika nodded, not looking up. She doubted this stranger meant what she said, but that wasn't important right now. Those were the words people said when they found out she was an orphan and were either trying to be polite or were pitying her, neither of which Tamika cared for, but both of which meant that her lie had been taken as truth.

And it wasn't a *total* lie. She really *was* an orphan.

The woman looked around again.

"Are you here all by yourself, then?" she asked.

Tamika nodded. "I just wanted to be alone," Tamika said, looking up at her, "And I'm living with my grandma now, and she's really old and pretty much blind and mostly deaf, so she couldn't have come anyway. I'm actually more taking care of her, really, it's like one of those situations, you know?"

Stop talking.

You already convinced them. Don't mess it up.

Like you always do.

Tamika clamped her mouth shut and ducked her head back down, but not before she saw a slow nod from the man.

"Jesse took care of his grandmother when he was

16

younger. It can be rough when you're just a kid," the woman said.

Again, Tamika nodded.

"My name's Mala Harwell, by the way," the woman said, holding her hand out to shake.

"Tamika," Tamika said, hesitating before taking the woman's much bigger hand. It was calloused and strong and a warm brown that probably seemed lighter than it was in comparison to Tamika's dark complexion. She had only ever known men with handshakes as firm as Mala's, except hers didn't hold the hint of a threat she'd always felt from the men who'd shaken her hand.

"And that's my husband, Jesse," Mala said, gesturing at him once she let go of Tamika's hand. Jesse waved, if the small raise and jerk of his hand could be called a wave, and maybe he smiled. It was hard to tell under his thick, dark beard at this distance. And the lime green polka-dot Band-Aid plastered across the bridge of his nose was drawing Tamika's attention. He would have made an imposing figure, if it hadn't been for that, and Tamika would have chuckled if they hadn't been strangers she was lying to. Or if she'd had the confidence to chuckle at an adult.

"Since we're here, we might as well have some lunch," Mala said, "What do you think, hon?"

Jesse nodded. Tamika still wasn't sure if he was smiling or not.

"Why don't you join us, kid?" Mala offered.

Tamika blinked. She'd hit Jesse with a rock, lied to both of them, and now they were asking her to join them for lunch? These were good people, really good people, and it made Tamika feel even worse.

"I dunno . . ." she said, looking down. She didn't deserve to be in their presence, to take any of their food. She deserved to be at the bottom of the river.

Disgusting.

"You don't have to if you don't want to," Mala said, pulling some food out of a bag, "but we really don't mind the company." She glanced at Jesse, who nodded, and turned back to smile at Tamika.

How could she say no to that?

A little voice in the back of her head screamed something about "stranger danger," but what did it matter now? If they were going to kidnap and kill her, it would only help her get to her goal that much quicker. She sat down on a blanket Jesse had spread out and took the sandwich Mala offered her. She ate slowly and carefully, not really tasting the food, in fear that Mala might offer her more. They didn't need to waste too much generosity on her.

"So, how'd you get all the way out here on your own?" Mala asked, "Your grandma doesn't sound like she's in any state to drive you."

"Uhm . . . I hitchhiked." A truth, finally.

"That's a bit dangerous, isn't it? Especially for a girl your age. You're, what, fourteen?"

"Fifteen," Tamika said. "It's fine."

Mala didn't look convinced. "Are you gonna be hitchhiking back?" she asked.

Not if you can stop being such a coward and jump in.

"Probably," Tamika said.

"You know, we've got a friend of ours on standby

with a car. We can call them up and they can give you a ride home."

"No!" Tamika said, maybe too fast and maybe too loud. She saw Jesse jump and Mala blink. She had to think of something to distract them from her mess-up. Something quick.

"So . . . uhm . . . what are you guys doing out here on the river?"

Mala smiled a gentle smile. "A source-to-sea trip," she said. "Do you know what that is?"

Tamika nodded. An old school friend of hers had a cousin who'd gone on one. The cousin had paddled from the source of the Missouri River, the longest river in the United States, through the Mississippi, and all the way down to where it emptied into the sea. Her school friend had bragged about it for months as if he, himself, had accomplished this feat, until one of the other kids had smacked him with a book. Tamika still wished that she had been bold enough to risk detention like that. It might have shut him up sooner.

"As a teacher, I've got summers off, and Jesse's been hoarding vacation days since forever," Mala said.

Jesse nodded.

"So we figured, why not? Let's do it just so we can say we did!"

Jesse scooted closer to Mala and took her hand, the fondness in his eyes clear.

Tamika managed a small smile, worrying that she'd put a damper on their adventure. From the source to the sea. Days and weeks and maybe months of nothing but the river and the wilderness. Tamika was sure she'd never be able to handle it. She could hardly handle normal life. She *couldn't* handle normal life, but if she couldn't get herself into the water before she was found out she'd have to go back to that life.

An idea began to take form.

A kayak could get her much closer to the water and shouldn't be too difficult to tip . . .

No. No, she'd already intruded on these strangers far too much. Throwing herself into the river from their kayak would only put even more of a damper on their mood.

This is why you should be dead.

But the way she'd been trying just wasn't working. Tamika hadn't been able to do it before the Harwells had shown up and she probably wouldn't be able to after they left. This was her only chance.

"So, uhm . . . it looks like you've got an extra seat there," she said.

Mala glanced back at the tandem kayak. "Oh, yeah. I guess you could call it that," she said.

Tamika didn't know what that meant, but she didn't really care. She was on a mission now. An awful mission, but one she would be punished for soon enough. She was the bad guy in this movie, and bad guys always got what they deserved. She worked up the courage to make the request that would probably ruin this couple's trip.

"Do you think . . . maybe I could fill it?"

Mala turned to her in confusion while Jesse looked at the kayak with a similar expression.

"Huh?" Mala asked.

"I mean, my parents . . . it would kind of be like honoring them, you know? And, like, you guys seem really good at kayaking and stuff, so I know I'd be, like, safe and, uh, me and my grandma can't afford a kayak, so, like . . . yeah. Can I?"

Mala gave her a look that made Tamika feel transparent, like she could see every lie, like she knew something more.

"Isn't your grandma expecting you home?" Mala said with a raised eyebrow.

"She won't mind!" Tamika said. Of course she wouldn't. She didn't exist. And even if she did, she wouldn't care about Tamika anyway. No one did.

"Why don't we call her and ask?" Mala said.

The problem of her grandma's nonexistence reared its head.

"Uhm . . . well . . . I don't have a phone . . . "

Mala pulled one out of her pocket and handed it to her.

"Thanks . . . " Tamika said in despair. Who was she

going to call? Her foster mother? Her social worker? Who wouldn't turn her in, stop her?

She felt another idea form and dialed the number she knew by heart.

"I swear to God, if this is those computer scam people again I will reach through the phone line and tear out your still beating heart!" said the voice on the other end of the line.

Tamika couldn't help but smile. Good old Bianca. Always full of fire. The closest thing Tamika had to someone who cared about her. She was one of the few friends that Tamika had managed to make moving from foster home to foster home. A year older than her, Bianca had been in the foster system herself before being adopted five years ago. Bianca understood. She cared. She had helped Tamika more times than Tamika could count and had always been ready with what was either the best or worst advice a person could give. Bianca was the only person who had never pitied her, not once, and Tamika hoped that she wouldn't be too upset at the news of her passing. At least she wouldn't be forcing her friend to sacrifice any more of her time and energy.

"Hi, Grandma!" Tamika said.

"Girl, I ain't no one's grandma! Who is this?"

"It's your granddaughter. You know, *Tamika*."

"Tami? What's going on? Why am I your grandma, all of a sudden?"

"Well, the person whose phone I'm borrowing and her husband are kayaking down the river, and I might be able to join them in my parents' honor. You know, 'cause of what happened to them on the river and all that? They said that I should get your permission, though."

"Can I speak with her?" Mala asked.

Tamika nodded. "Mrs. Harwell wants to speak with you, Grandma," she said. "Is that okay? I know you don't like talking on the phone because your hearing isn't as good as it used to be."

"Oooo, girl, give her the phone! Imma have fun with this!" This worried Tamika somewhat, but she trusted Bianca. She handed the phone to Mala.

"Hello? Ma'am, my name is Mala Harwell. May I start off by saying that I'm so sorry for your loss . . . " She paused to listen to what Tamika's "grandmother" had to say and then in a louder voice said, "I SAID, I'M SORRY FOR YOUR LOSS! . . . Yes, right, so Tamika was wondering if she could kayak down the river with us to honor her parents. I thought you might . . . I SAID, SHE WANTS TO KAYAK DOWN THE . . . Oh, okay. Don't you want to meet me and my husband first? . . . Are you *sure*, ma'am? . . . I SAID, ARE YOU SURE?" Mala paused, blinking at whatever Bianca said next.

Tamika held her breath, certain that Mala had just realized she was speaking with a sixteen-year-old rather than an eighty-year-old.

Instead, Mala turned to Jesse and smiled. "Why, yes, I do believe he's very handsome."

Tamika could only imagine what Bianca had said to get that reaction, but she didn't dare to. She couldn't just burst into laughter now.

Mala, on the other hand, could and did. She stood listening for a long stretch.

"That's such a sweet story, ma'am!" she said, finally, and then louder, "I SAID, THAT WAS VERY SWEET! . . . Yes, it's been wonderful speaking with you. If you're certain . . . I SAID, IF YOU'RE . . . Oh, yes, you can speak with her." Mala handed the phone back to Tamika.

"Hello?"

"How was that, young whippersnapper?" Bianca said in her best old lady voice.

"Thanks so much, Grandma!" Tamika said with a smile.

"You're darn right! Respect your elders! Ha!" Bianca sounded as pleased with herself as she'd been that time she scammed Dylan Hoff into doing all her homework for her. "Hope you have a good time, Tami! Don't do anything stupid," she laughed.

"Yeah. Yeah, I won't." Tamika's stomach dropped. If things went the way she had planned, this was prob-ably the last time she was going to speak to her best friend. These were her last words to her. She could feel a lump in her throat.

"I love you," Tamika said. Bianca just laughed, as if this was just a normal goodbye on a normal phone call. As if Tamika would be dialing the numbers she knew by heart on another phone someday. As if she was going to take Bianca's advice.

"Love you, too, Tami!" Bianca made a smooching sound on the other end of the line and hung up. Tamika stared at the phone in her hand for a few seconds too long, forcing her emotions deep inside herself and locking them away. Having emotions, especially strong ones, had never ended well for her.

"Tamika?" Mala asked.

Tamika looked up at her concerned face, then quickly looked back down and handed her the phone. "Thank you," she said.

Mala took the phone and gave Tamika a long, searching look. She turned that look to the phone, then sighed as if some big decision had been made.

"Alright," she said, smiling at Tamika, "Good thing we brought that spare life jacket. Let's see if it fits you."

Chapter Three

THERE WAS A GLARING FLAW IN TAMIKA'S PLAN, something anyone other than her would have realized in a second: she had never kayaked before. She had never been on a boat of any kind. Was her weight going to throw Mala off? Was it going to tip the second she climbed in? How was she even supposed to sit in that thing? The hole looked so small. She was supposed to be from a family who had died kayaking! How was she going to keep that lie up without her lack of skill giving her away?

Tamika clipped on the life jacket Mala had given her and watched Mala as she got into her part of the kayak. She took a deep breath and tried to copy the woman's movements, letting it out when she found that the kayak was more stable than she had thought. Though she wasn't about to put that to the test just yet.

Mala handed her an oar with a paddle on each end and pushed off the shore.

Tamika watched her as she paddled, then tried to copy the motions. Jesse paddled up next to her. Tamika froze. Was he going to ask her something? Was he already suspicious? But he just continued to paddle at a pace that matched Mala's kayak, pausing to watch Tamika every few strokes, making the motions more exaggerated when she didn't move.

He was trying to teach her.

She started to copy his motions, trying to get each paddle to enter the water without any splash like Jesse was. She was so focused, she almost didn't catch the little upward twitch of his lips.

"How's it feel, kid?" Mala asked.

"Pretty good." One more truth.

31

"Great! Feel free to take any breaks you need!"

Tamika nodded and Mala pushed forward, Jesse by their side.

- - -

Tamika did her best to keep up with the Harwells' pace, not wanting to slow Mala down. Difficult as it was, she found that she didn't mind. In fact, she was enjoying the push, the burn of her muscles, the feel of the wind. She'd never had much opportunity to work out aside from mandatory gym classes. School sports cost money that her foster families had never been willing to shell out. Besides, between school work and the stress of trying to prove to herself and everyone else that she was worth something, she hadn't given working out much thought. Maybe she should have. She felt better than she had in a while.

She could see Jesse getting away from them, though. Despite her effort and Jesse's lesson, she was slowing Mala down.

Mala noticed. She stopped and signaled for Jesse to come back and join them.

"You doing alright, back there?" Mala asked.

"Fine. Good. I can keep up. It's fine," Tamika said between pants. When had she gotten this winded?

"You know, it's okay if you can't. We don't mind slowing down the pace."

Jesse nodded.

"And you can take breaks, remember? You're a kid. We're adults and we've been doing this for *years*. Seriously, it's okay."

Jesse knocked on the back of the tandem and pointed at the sky. When she looked up, she saw a hawk circling overhead. No, that was an eagle! As Tamika stared, it landed in a tree and let out a caw.

"And Jesse's right," Mala said, "The scenery is beautiful. Can't see that too clearly when you're going super fast."

As Mala spoke, Tamika's eyes followed the eagle. It pulled her gaze to the tops of the trees, dark green against the blue sky, climbing up the sides of cliffs.

Ahead, a wall of the cascading pines blocked her view of the river's curve. At least, she guessed they were pines. That was what she could see around her, so the distant green must be similar. Grass and shrubs and wildflowers crept close to the water's edge, soaking up the drink it offered. Sand and stones (good skipping stones) were even closer to the water, smaller versions of some of the large rocks she saw dotting the river, making the water move faster between them. No rapids, yet. Nothing that couldn't be paddled around. Above, the sky was as endless as a cliché, framed by the tops of the trees and cliffs. Wispy clouds and jet tracks moved across it.

It was beautiful.

Tamika was beginning to enjoy herself.

Mala pointed out the rocks in the river. "Be careful of those," she said, "You see the way the water moves around the rock? Those are called eddies and they're the main indicator that something's in the way, even if you can't see it."

"Like rapids?"

"Not exactly. There really aren't that many rapids on this river, but we might come across a few, or at least something as dangerous and difficult to navigate. But don't you worry about a thing. Jesse and I will help you out. We've been doing this since we were kids."

Jesse nodded.

Tamika didn't know how she felt about this, so she went back to enjoying the scenery.

Chapter Four

THE DAY WAS A COMBINATION OF SILENT LESSONS
from Jesse and loud ones from Mala, mixed in
with plenty of nature appreciation. It was enough to
distract Tamika from her initial goal, and by the end of
the day, she was only a little disappointed at that.

*Good job, learning how to not tip over and drown,
genius. You're making this harder on yourself.*

Of course, *that* voice still wouldn't shut up.

But now they had to set up camp and Tamika could
shove it away a little longer. She had never camped
before, but she'd watched the patented "Camping
Episode" on a million different TV shows and she'd

heard classmates' stories. She'd always wanted those fun mishaps for herself.

She watched Jesse unpack a bag: canvas, poles, pegs. It had to be the tent. She wondered if she would fit. The Harwells had set out thinking it would be just the two of them. What if she had to sleep outside? With no protection whatsoever? Or, worse, what if Mala or Jesse volunteered to in her place?

"You ever camped before?" Mala asked.

Tamika shook her head, banishing the thoughts and indicating that she hadn't simultaneously.

"Great! Jesse's got someone to teach, then!" She wrapped her arms around her husband who turned to kiss her cheek. Mala giggled. Tamika didn't think that she had ever heard a grown woman giggle in real life before.

"I'm going to head into town, get some gear for you, Tamika, and get a burn permit. It's not a real campsite without a campfire!" She turned to leave, ruffling Tamika's hair as she passed, which surprised

Tamika so much that she forgot to protest Mala buying her anything until she was too far away.

Jesse gave Tamika's shoulder a light tap. When she turned, she saw that he was holding up the tent poles.

"You want me to help with the tent?" she asked.

He nodded.

Tamika looked down.

"You . . . probably don't want that. I'm not good at stuff like this. I'll just mess it up . . . "

Jesse held a tent pole in her direction, insistent. She hesitated before taking it, hand shaking a little, hoping she wasn't going to disappoint him. Mishaps were only delightful and quirky on TV.

— — —

Jesse's actions did most of the talking. As they set up the tent, he would demonstrate the right way to do things, then step aside to give Tamika a chance. She would try and he would either nod once with a smile or correct her with gestures and more demonstrations.

He was gentle and he was patient. He never got angry with her, even when she accidentally ripped part of the tent wall. He just shook his head, got out a roll of duct tape, and showed her how to fix it.

Tamika had never had a teacher like him before, someone who made sure she was learning, who cared if she was. With him, silence didn't feel like a cement block of awkwardness trying to crush her. It felt . . . comfortable. Amicable. It was nice.

On some level, it made her feel worse about hitting him with that rock. She hadn't done it on purpose, but the lime green polka-dot Band-Aid was accusing, even if Jesse's expression wasn't. Her eyes were drawn to it, such a loud statement against his dark skin. She tried to refocus her attention on the tent whenever she felt that she had been staring at it for too long.

Not long after they finished, Mala came back holding a shopping bag in each hand.

"The burn permit is in there," she said handing one of the bags to Jesse, "And some gear for the lady." She handed the other bag to Tamika. "Let me know if it fits. I'm going for the world record for guessing people's sizes."

Tamika thanked her, forgetting to chuckle at the joke until it was too late and ducked into the tent to try things on. Inside of the bag were four changes of clothes: two T-shirts, two tank tops, four pairs of shorts, five pairs of socks and underwear (even underwear!), a baseball cap, a water bottle (already filled), and a blanket. The shorts and shirts were made of Dri-FIT and just her size. This stuff *had* to be expensive, but Mala had already removed all the tags, so Tamika couldn't tell. Why would someone, practically a stranger, spend money like that on her? Did Mala just feel sorry for her? It had to be that. There was no other reason anyone but Bianca had ever done anything nice for her. She changed back into her regular clothes and walked out of the tent to see Mala's expectant face.

"Well?" she asked.

Tamika looked down at the bag. "It all fits really well . . . " she said.

Mala pumped a fist in the air and high-fived Jesse. Another tally for whoever kept track of world records.

"But you really didn't have to buy all this for me," Tamika said.

"What? Nonsense!" Mala said, waving her concerns away. "You need a few changes of clothes if you're going all the way to the sea with us, and you need ones that'll work for kayaking, and I had this gift card that I'd been wanting to use, anyway, so don't you go worrying your pretty little head about it, m'kay?"

Tamika's concerns weren't waved away with Mala's fast-paced excuses and explanations. She still had questions. Questions that she wasn't able to form into words. Some involved the reason the Harwells had agreed to bring her with them and some went deeper, involving her lies and her initial plan. Her resolve had faded a little over the day, and she wasn't sure what to think or feel about that.

Instead of asking any of those questions, she just thanked them again.

"You're welcome, kid. Now! Let me show you how to make an awesome campfire!"

– – –

Tamika stared into the roaring campfire, hugging her knees to her chest, finishing off a post-dinner s'more. She hadn't realized how hungry she had been until they had started to cook the food, and then she'd devoured it. This had amused the Harwells and embarrassed Tamika, so she'd roasted her marshmallows in silence with the stick Mala had helped her find and tried to find a topic for small talk.

"So, what's with the tandem kayak, anyway?" Tamika asked with her mouth full. She paused, remembering almost every foster parent she'd had reprimanding her for talking with her mouth full, swallowed, and started again. "Sorry, why do you guys have a tandem kayak? You don't have three people."

Mala chuckled. Tamika pulled her legs a little

closer to her chest, embarrassed once again. Was Mala making fun of her? Probably not, but maybe . . .

"Jesse, should I tell her?" Mala asked.

Jesse gave Tamika a long, searching look, then nodded.

"Jesse has moments, sometimes days, when he can't do the paddling on his own. It could be because he's overtired or just overwhelmed, all of his senses giving his brain too much information to handle. The tandem helps by giving him the option to take breaks."

Jesse nodded along as she spoke.

Tamika was confused. That didn't sound like something that could happen to grown-ups. Even kids, herself included, were told to suck it up when they felt like that.

"You see, kiddo," Mala continued, "a lot of the time, when he's feeling like that, he can't physically or mentally function enough to paddle or fight the current, or navigate a tricky spot. It's part of the way his autism works."

Autism? Tamika didn't know much about autism.

She didn't think she'd ever even met anyone who had it. She *had* seen some characters in shows and movies, but Jesse didn't act much like them.

Jesse straightened his back and puffed out his chest, proud. Tamika didn't understand why.

Mala seemed to, though. She hugged him. "Which is part of the reason we worked so hard to go on this trip. A lot of people told Jesse that he'd never be able to do it because he's autistic. He wants to prove them wrong and I want to help him."

Jesse nodded and it started to make sense to Tamika, as well.

"I'm really glad we're doing this," Mala said to Jesse. "I'm really proud of you."

Jesse hugged her back and they were just so adorable in that moment that Tamika couldn't help but ask, "How did you guys meet?"

Jesse's face lit up. He pulled away from the hug and made several rapid hand motions. Tamika squinted, her mouth slightly open, trying to decipher the meaning.

Mala chuckled again. "I don't think she understands sign language, hon," she said.

Sign language? Why would Jesse be using sign language? She was almost one-hundred-percent positive that he wasn't deaf. He'd responded plenty of times when she or Mala had spoken to him. Maybe he could read lips? But, no, he'd also responded while he was turned away from them. Was he mute? She hadn't heard him speak. Had someone cut out his tongue or done something to his voice?

Maybe it had something to do with his autism? That seemed most likely. Most of the autistic characters she'd seen could talk, but Jesse had already proven that they weren't exactly the best indicator of what autistic people are really like.

He raised his eyebrows at Mala and moved his hand to indicate the both of them a few times insistently.

"Of course, of course," Mala said, then turned back to Tamika. "He said that the Scouts was actually where we met."

Jesse wrapped his arms around Mala's arm and

rested his head on her shoulder, watching her like she was the most important thing in his world.

"I was seventeen," Mala began, "a year away from leaving the Girl Scout troop I'd grown up with, a year away from college or a gap year, I hadn't decided yet, and I was gonna milk it for everything it was worth. When my troop decided to go on a camping trip with three other troops before school started, I was ecstatic. I don't think I'd ever packed so fast or so early. It was, like, a week before the trip and my bags were at the door." She laughed and Jesse snorted.

"The trip was a blast. We even had a final fire party with the Boy Scout troop that was camping a few miles north of us. We were having the time of our lives, barring a few cases of poison ivy and bee stings—except for one person." She turned to look at Jesse. "He was always by himself, away from the group, refusing to sleep in the same tent as anyone else, not wanting to go on the hikes or swim with anyone else.

"The guys from his troop insisted that he was 'just like that,' that he was 'quiet and weird,' and 'no fun to be around, anyway.' I, of course, didn't listen. I wanted everyone to have as much fun as I was having.

"Before the night was over, I went over to him and tried to start up a conversation.

"I said, 'Hi! I'm Mala! What's your name?' or something, even though the other guys had already told me his name.

"He just stared at me and said nothing.

"I asked him why he was sitting there all by himself and he kind of glared at . . . or it was more of a disdainful glance, really . . . he disdainfully glanced at the guys from his troop, so I guessed that he didn't like them much, and he was all surprised that I had understood."

Jesse nodded. Tamika wondered how much it took for him to get people to understand him.

"I still wanted him to have as much fun as us, so I started listing things."

Jesse signed something and Mala giggled.

"Yeah, it started out as regular old camping junk

and it just got ridiculous from there. I was trying to get him to laugh."

Jesse let out a silent giggle and Mala smiled.

"Yeah! Like that! I think you really started laughing when I mentioned something about a woodpecker . . ."

Jesse signed something.

"Right, right! Catch a woodpecker, have it whittle us a flute, and then use that flute to summon fairies."

Tamika was trying to keep her own laughter in.

"Yeah, that one really cracked him up," Mala said. "Then he started to sign at me, but stopped. He stopped laughing, too. I don't know why. I think it's neat that he uses sign language. It led to me learning sign language."

He signed something again.

"What?" Tamika asked.

"He said that not everyone thinks like that," said Mala.

"Well, I think it's pretty neat, too," Tamkia said. Jesse smiled at her. The laughter must have made him more comfortable with her. She was a little more certain that his signing had something to do with his autism, but her earlier embarrassment kept her from asking. Besides, she didn't want to say the wrong thing and make them hate her, something she knew would happen if she opened her mouth again. She wanted to hear the rest of the story.

"So, since I didn't speak sign language yet, we started communicating with this journal he'd brought along. We became such good friends that he even let me look through it. It was full of all these myths and legends and cryptids—you know, like Bigfoot and stuff. If you need fairy lore, Jesse's your guy."

Jesse nodded, his hands twitching and patting his legs as if he was dying to talk about them.

"Sometime after that summer and between hand-written letters and fairy hunts, we fell in love." Mala touched her forehead to her husband's and they closed their eyes. It was one of the sweetest things that Tamika had seen between two real-life adults, but there was one thing about the story that didn't quite make sense.

"So, why was Jesse sitting all by himself in the first place?" she asked. There had to be an interesting story behind that, and Tamika was already in love with the way Mala told stories.

Mala pulled away from Jesse a little, giving him a questioning glance. He nodded.

"Well, Jesse was severely bullied when he was growing up," Mala said. "He could never stand up for himself because of his condition, and the problem grew worse the older he got."

Suddenly, the situation felt delicate again. Being bullied was a topic Tamika knew all too well.

"So . . . nobody cut out his tongue?"

Shut up, just SHUT UP.

"Wait, what?" Mala asked, confused.

Tamika flinched internally. Wrong thing. Always the wrong thing.

Stupid. You could've kept your mouth shut!

"No, nobody cut out his tongue," Mala continued,

"he's always been naturally quiet around people. He likes to feel them out before he decides he's comfortable enough to chat. And when a person turns out to be a giant jerk, good luck getting a peep from him at all."

Jesse nodded. Mala smiled. Neither of them looked mad. In fact, they seemed glad they could teach her something. What a strange feeling.

"Oh," Tamika said, "so that's why you were so uncomfortable there. Because they were giant jerks!"

Jesse signed something and Mala burst into laughter.

"What?" Tamika asked, a small smile of her own forming. Mala's laughter was contagious.

"Apparently," she said between giggles, "apparently they were also 'a bunch of losers.'"

Jesse made an L-shape with his finger and his thumb and put it to his forehead, a sign even Tamika understood. She started to laugh, too. She hadn't messed up, she hadn't hurt their feelings.

They didn't hate her.

The fire crackled and the crickets chirped. Cicadas buzzed in the quiet leaves of the trees surrounding them. Over all this, the trio laughed. Tamika could just barely hear the sound of the river rushing, running through the night without a thought of rest. The stars were brighter than she had ever seen them and not just because her mood had turned. There was no light pollution out here. Nothing in the way of their beauty.

And here she was: alive and enjoying herself with two people who loved each other and didn't hate her.

Maybe her plan could wait a little longer.

Chapter Five

*T*AMIKA WAS UNDERWATER, BUT SHE WASN'T DROWNING. *Breathing felt strange. The space surrounding her was a deep, dark, empty blue. Gravity was meaningless.*

Jesse swam by, the green polka-dot Band-Aid on his nose glowing like a headlight. It began to grow. Bigger and bigger and bigger until it swallowed him. He struggled within it, silently thrashing until he couldn't. She watched the bubbles trail him as he sank into the devouring blackness that the dark blue faded into.

Tamika tried to get to him, but she couldn't move. The water was too thick, too crushing.

Useless.

Mala swam past, after Jesse, a desperate, devastated look on her face. She glared at Tamika before diving deeper, no trace of her usual smile anywhere.

Pathetic.

Tamika tried to scream, to move, to do something.

The world started to shake. She could hear words, muffled, saying . . .

– – –

"Time to get up, kid!"

Tamika stared up at Mala's bright smile. A dream. A nightmare. That was all it had been. She took a deep breath and laid an arm across her eyes, feeling sick.

"What time is it?" she mumbled.

"Five in the morning," Mala said.

Tamika lifted her arm to stare at Mala. She had to be kidding. Mala's smile only grew despite the fact that there wasn't even light streaking through the walls of the tent and despite the fact that her hair was a disheveled, frizzy mess. Tamika had a feeling that her own hair was no better. Mala tugged on Tamika's arm.

"Come on," she said, "we're packing up the camp. We're gonna try and get the kayaks in before sunrise."

As Mala left, Tamika dragged herself up, suppressing a groan. She was tired. She was sore. She was sweaty. As much as she had tried to carve out her own little corner in the tent, it was still only meant for two people and it had still been cramped. Tamika could remember there being no way for her to not be touching at least one of them, but she had also been so tired that she hadn't cared.

She was still tired. But if the Harwells wanted her up, she was going to get up. She just had to keep her eyes from closing again. She was usually only awake this early in the morning because she had lost track of time and stayed up all night watching TV.

She ran a hand through her hair and it stuck. She didn't have any relaxers or straighteners, or even a brush. What was she supposed to do with this mess?

She could see the disapproving looks of every foster mother she'd ever had.

She smacked her cheeks a few times and shook her head in an attempt to banish the exhaustion that still hung around her. Pulling the blanket off, she dragged herself over to her bag of new clothes. It was still hard to believe that Mala had bought all of this for her. After changing, she walked out of the tent to see the Harwells packing up the camp, rolling things up into waterproof casings and stuffing them either into the bags strapped to the kayaks or the hollow spaces in the front and back.

When Jesse spotted her, he walked over and began to show her how to take down the tent. She did the best she could as every blink threatened to turn into a nap. At some point, she noticed that Jesse's Band-Aid had changed. It was no longer bright green with polka dots, but clear. She stared at it for longer than she probably should have, her brain taking longer than usual to process the change. It felt significant, somehow.

After a few moments of this, Jesse itched at the Band-Aid and turned away. Tamika blinked and shook her head. She needed to snap out of it. It took her at least an hour to wake herself up in the mornings, which was not good for early classes. She tried rubbing the sleep out of her eyes and brushing the hair out of her face. Ugh. It was *everywhere*.

Mala nudged her arm. Tamika looked to see that she was holding out a scrunchie.

"You look like you might need one," she said. Tamika took it, pulling her hair back into a ponytail.

"Sorry," she said, "it's just so nappy . . . "

"That's alright," Mala said, "so long as most of it's not in your face, it doesn't matter much." She pointed to her own hair. "Takes a lot of time off getting ready." She chuckled. "Besides, it looks pretty cute like that."

Tamika touched her hair with a small smile, then turned back to help finish the packing.

– – –

Mala looked at her watch.

"Packed and ready with ten minutes to spare! Record!" she said. She held her hand up and Jesse high-fived her, then she held both of her hands down towards Tamika. Tamika smiled and low-fived her.

"Thanks for the extra set of hands. Now, come on!" She pushed their kayak into the river. "You're gonna want to see the sunrise from the water! It's incredible!" She giggled, excitement pouring off of her.

Jesse handed Tamika her life jacket and helped her into the boat before getting into his own.

The sky had turned a lighter blue as they were packing, the change so gradual that Tamika's tired mind hadn't noticed until now. The moment the sun peeked over the horizon, spreading a band of pinkish orange upwards, she gasped. It reflected on the water, a long, yellow spike of light shooting out, then growing smaller as the sun rose into its proper position. The few clouds that were out were tinged with the same pinkish orange as the horizon, and the light fog that hung in the air shone in a such way that Tamika expected to be able to reach out and feel it. Everything was glowing. The chill of the night evaporated, her skin growing warmer every minute.

"Do you guys just . . . get up to watch this, every day?" Tamika asked.

"Most days," Mala said, her arms hanging off the paddle that rested on her shoulders. "I mean, sometimes I just can't force myself to get up that early." She laughed. "But Jesse never misses it."

Jesse was watching the sky, not paying attention to either of them. His smile was more apparent than Tamika had ever seen it. Mala watched him watching the sunrise. Tamika was sure that, if she asked, Mala would say that he was her sunrise or something sappy like that. But Tamika didn't ask. She just pulled her new cap on and began paddling towards the horizon.

"Gonna start with pushing me today, huh?" Mala asked with a chuckle. "Always wanted a chauffeur."

Tamika laughed. As they passed by Jesse's kayak, Mala tapped it with her oar.

"You're it!" she shouted, then started to paddle.

Jesse blinked, then smirked, then went after them.

"Tag team, Tamika! You and me!" Mala said, laughing at her own alliteration.

Tamika laughed harder, adrenaline and joy working together to make her feel like she was floating, not just in the water, but somewhere in her mind.

The game went on for the better part of four miles, as much of a work out as it was fun. Tamika and Mala made a good team, one of them reaching out to tag Jesse as the other paddled. Jesse had to get creative in order to either tag or avoid them. They were all breathing heavily when they decided to take a break.

Tamika's stomach growled. It must've been loud, because Jesse pulled an energy bar out of his bag and handed it to her. She accepted it with haste.

"You didn't eat anything this morning, did you, kid?" Mala said. Tamika paused, then shook her head. She always felt too sick to eat in the early morning and she had been too tired to focus on anything other than packing the camp. The sunrise and the game had distracted her after that.

"I'm sorry," Mala said. "I forget to eat in the morning, too. I should've thought about you."

"It's okay," Tamika muttered. It wasn't like people hadn't forgotten to feed her before.

"Let us know next time, okay?" Mala said. "Don't want you passing out in the middle of the river and drowning."

Tamika finished her energy bar as quickly and quietly as she was able to.

"You know what? You've actually given me an idea!" Mala said. She reached into the front of the kayak and pulled out what looked like a very short fishing pole. Jesse pointed and nodded, reaching into the front of his and pulling out his own. When he expanded it, Tamika realized that it wasn't just a short fishing pole, it was a collapsible one. She didn't even know that they made those.

"You ever fished before, Tamika?" Mala asked.

"Uh, once."

It had been boring and frustrating. One of Tamika's foster fathers had taken her to attempt some kind of bonding. He had gone on and on about how it was usually a father-son kind of thing, how he'd never had a foster *daughter* before, and how to do every itty-bitty little detail several times with the most condescending smile Tamika had ever seen in her life, never mind that she had understood the first time he'd said it. She hadn't lasted long at that house.

Jesse was shaking his head. Was he trying to say that he didn't believe her? Was he going to smile that same condescending smile she couldn't stand but couldn't bring herself to say anything about?

He nodded his head to indicate Mala, who was already struggling with the fishing line with concentration and excitement.

"Ow! Dangit," she said, pricking her finger on the hook, and then tried to work out whatever problem she was having from another angle. "Ow! Dangit," she said again, pricking her finger a second time. Sucking on that finger, she continued to struggle with one hand, her enthusiasm unsullied.

Jesse turned to Tamika and wiggled his eyebrows.

Oh.

She may have fished before, but she hadn't really experienced it until she'd seen Mala attempt to fish.

Mala pricked the same finger again. Jesse handed Tamika his pole and pulled their boat over to him, untangling the wire.

"Thanks, hon!" she said, kissing him on the cheek. She cast her line, catching Tamika's hat and throwing it out with the hook in the process.

"Got something!" She reeled the hat back in and plopped it back onto Tamika's head with a smile. "Sorry about that."

Tamika waved her away with a relieved smile. The cold water seeping through her hair and dripping onto her face felt amazing in this heat, especially after so much paddling.

As Tamika watched her, she realized that Mala was excellent at the "catching" part, but not so much at the "fish" part of "catching fish." Her grand, arcing casts caught a tree branch, the shore, and the kayaks, all before Tamika had a chance to cast the line Jesse had loaned her. Jesse, while seeming content to watch Mala do her thing, gave Tamika a few subtle hints on improving her technique whenever he checked on her.

Mala's antics kept boredom from setting in while they waited for the fish to bite. It also might have kept the fish from biting, but that didn't matter as much.

An hour later, Tamika felt a tug at her line. Could it be . . . ? Another tug and the reel started spinning. Tamika grabbed it, reeling it in the opposite direction.

"Ahhh!" Mala shouted when she saw. She dropped her rod—which Jesse picked up—and turned to Tamika, rocking the boat in the process.

"You got one! You got one! Reel it in! Reel it in!" she cheered.

Tamika *was* reeling. The fish wasn't fighting her much, but it was harder to keep her balance in the kayak than on the shore, especially with Mala's excitement making it move. Out of the corner of her eye, she could see Jesse trying to tell her something, but was too focused on balancing and reeling to give him her attention.

Then the kayak tipped. She felt a rush of fear as a spark of her nightmare flickered into her mind's eye. With a splash and a shock to her system, she was in the river. The water was colder than she had expected.

"Tamika! Are you alright?" Mala shouted, spluttering and splashing towards her.

She wasn't going under? The life jacket! Right, of course. She didn't feel the same disappointment she'd felt at the missed opportunity of the other day.

She nodded at Mala, who let out a breath.

"Oh, good. Grab the back of my jacket, I'll get you to shore," she said. Tamika did so, embarrassed. That had probably been what Jesse had been trying to tell her, but she'd ignored him and dunked Mala in for her trouble.

Stupid.

"I'm sorry," Tamika said when they got to shore.

"What are you sorry for? I fall off of that thing fishing all the time! At least you actually had a fish on your line." Mala laughed. After seeing the way that Mala "fished," it was hard not to laugh with her.

"You didn't get a hook anywhere, did you?" Mala asked, checking her over.

"I don't think so . . . the fishing pole! I dropped it!" She moved to retrieve it, but Jesse was already there, holding both the pole she'd dropped and the pole that Mala had dropped in one hand and a fish on a line in the other.

"You caught it," Tamika said.

Jesse shook his head and pointed at her.

"What? No, I fell off! You're the one with the fish."

"Maybe, but you're the one who got it on the line in the first place," Mala said. "That's most of the battle, right there. Now! Seeing as we're all washed up and fish-ified, I say we cook ourselves up some early lunch, caveman-style. Come, my loyal assistant!" She turned and started walking towards a patch of trees, steps squelching from the water in her shoes. Tamika followed.

"We're gonna make a fire?" Tamika asked. "Don't we need a burning permit or something? Like last time?"

"Well, last time we were on a public campground. Had to pay for the spot and everything. This time, we're not, and we'll be close enough to the river that there won't be much of a fire hazard. I won't tell if you won't tell." She winked.

Tamika smiled. None of her foster families had ever suggested that they would do something even slightly illegal. Some of them would even condemn downloading *music* illegally, and that was how everyone she knew got their music! She was sure it had something to do with being good role models, like a requirement for foster parents or something. But maybe she was wrong to feel a small thrill at the idea of an adult encouraging lawbreaking, even if it was something small like this.

She felt it anyway.

— — —

The fish—*her* fish, the Harwells insisted—was delicious, which came as a surprise. Something someone had said about "dirty river water" had stuck with her years ago, so she had expected the fish to be dirty, as well.

Mala had shown her how to kill, scale, gut, and clean it while Jesse stood a few steps away with his back turned. Tamika had to admit that part had made her feel a bit squeamish, too, but Mala's expert handling had made it easier to bear. Jesse had rejoined them for the cooking portion, bringing with him some kind of metal grate that made the campfire into a makeshift grill. As they all picked at it from the plate, Tamika thought she had never tasted anything so fresh.

Getting back on the river was a lot more pleasant with more in her stomach. She could focus again, a problem she hadn't realized she'd been having until it was gone.

Her soreness was even starting to fade. The more she moved, the better she felt. It didn't make sense—she'd been so stiff in the morning—but it was happening and she wasn't willing to question it too much.

She didn't have to question anything as long as she

was moving, as long as she had more of the river to see. She paddled. She felt the water pull at her oar, she felt the wind on her face, she felt the burn in her muscles, she felt the splashes of water that landed on her lap (much more often than the Harwells, whose laps were practically dry). She felt the sun on her face, drying the clothes that she hadn't bothered to change after falling in. She felt its heat and she felt herself sweat from working so hard in it. But she didn't think. She was nothing more than a physical being, a mindless paddling machine.

"Hey, Tamika?" Mala said.

Why was Mala stopping her? She was on a roll!

"Kid, it's getting dark. We should make camp."

. . . Oh. That was why. She hadn't noticed. Time flies when you've pushed all coherent thought to the side!

She paddled in with them and helped set up camp. She did more than she had last time, keeping herself busy and moving until she absolutely *had* to sit down. She could tell that Jesse was proud of her.

Okay, "proud" was a strong word. A word she never used because she was sure that she was not someone to be proud of. He was probably more impressed, or maybe just surprised. Yeah. One of those worked. At least she was being useful instead of dead weight. At least doing something kept her thoughts occupied.

They had baked beans for dinner and s'mores for dessert.

"It's not a campfire without s'mores," Mala said, "And it's not a *true* campfire without a *spooky story*." She wiggled her fingers, still sticky with marshmallow goop.

The s'more turned to rock in Tamika's throat. She swallowed a few times, refusing to choke on it. She didn't like scary stories. She could *handle* them; she had watched plenty of horror movies to know that. She'd had friends and foster siblings who loved them and—in order to prove that she was not the little crybaby they made fun of her for being—she would sit through them and pretended she wasn't terrified.

She considered telling Mala that she would prefer

there to be no spooky stories. She'd had a nightmare the other night and didn't want to suffer through another, but Mala had already said that a *true* campfire had spooky stories, and Jesse looked excited. She was going to have to suck it up, feeling like an intruder on their fun.

Mala thought for a moment while licking the remaining marshmallow off of her fingers, deciding which story would be best to tell.

"Once," she began, "a *looooooong* time ago, the river belonged to a woman. It was calm and flowed gently, provided for humans without a fuss. Of course, humans had to ask permission from the woman before they could take anything from the river, or use it at all. She didn't require offerings. All she wanted was for them to ask nicely and not take more than they needed. But the humans got greedy. They wanted to take whatever they wanted whenever they wanted, no matter what the woman said."

Mala lowered her voice, as if telling them a secret.

"One night, a group of humans snuck into her tent

while she was asleep and kidnapped her. They tied her to four heavy rocks—one for each limb—and threw her into her river. The shock of hitting the icy water woke her and she struggled against her bonds." Mala mimed struggling. "But no matter how much she thrashed, she couldn't escape." She stopped moving. "When the people saw the bubbles stop, they knew the river no longer belonged to her."

Tamika hugged her legs to her chest, trembling. Mala returned to her normal voice.

"The humans could do what they wanted, now, but the woman's thrashing had made the current rushed and rocky, forming rapids too treacherous to cross. It swallowed the humans who had killed its owner—the justice of nature—and continues to swallow those who refuse to take precaution. In a way, people still needed to ask the River Woman's permission."

Mala paused for what Tamika assumed was dramatic effect.

"As for the woman, she remains in the river. They say that you can still see her shadow in the trees while you're on the water. That, in calm spots, you can look down and see her reflection. That she comes to people about to drown, sits beside them in their tents, stares, dripping, and whispers about the age-old debt that must still be paid."

Tamika didn't like the sound of any of that. There was no way the story was true, but she still asked, in a hushed tone, "Is . . . is all that true?"

"Truer than true," Mala said, leaning closer to the flames, their light throwing creepy shadows on her face.

Jesse shook his head and said something in sign language.

"I do *not* make things up!" Mala said. "Every word I say is one-hundred-percent *true* all the time!" She leaned back, folded her arms, and turned her nose towards the sky.

Jesse rolled his eyes. Tamika forced a chuckle. True or not, she had curled herself into a tight ball of fear. She blamed the darkness of the forest, the flickering campfire light, and the muffled sound of the river. That River Woman was going to show up in her nightmares, she knew it. Monsters and ghosts always did.

Jesse took a small notebook out of his pocket. He wrote in it, then handed it to Tamika.

"If you spoke sign language, I could tell you a better story! One that's based on actual lore from the area we're in. That would be truer than whatever Mala can come up with," it said.

"Well, I guess I'll have to learn sign language," Tamika said.

I'm glad I don't know sign language, she thought.

"What did he say?" Mala asked, walking over to read over Tamika's shoulder. When she finished, she flicked Jesse in the head. He chuckled silently.

Tamika forced another smile. Maybe the Harwells' cheerfulness would be enough to banish the ghosts.

Chapter Six

DEEP, DARK BLUE AND FREEZING COLD. SHE COULD breathe, but she couldn't move. Familiar.

Something colder grabbed her ankle. A pale hand, the skin so white it was almost translucent. Her eyes ran down the length of the arm to the emaciated face of a woman with long, black hair that splayed in every direction and blended into the deep blue background. Her staring eyes were filmed over and her mouth was agape. She didn't move unless Tamika tried to struggle and then only to tighten her grip.

She was dragging Tamika down.

Tamika looked up. Light shone through the surface

of the water and Mala and Jesse laughed above it. Tamika tried to reach up, to swim towards them, but the woman kept dragging her down. She tried to scream, but could force no sound out. No matter what she did, the woman dragged her farther and farther into the blackness . . .

– – –

Tamika paddled harder than she had the other day. The nightmare clung to her like the stiff, icy fingers of the dead woman had clung to her ankle. The burn in her muscles didn't burn the memory of it away, only blunted the edges a bit.

She rowed harder, angrier. Mala turned to her with a concerned look.

"Hey, kid, are you alright?" she asked, "You're attacking the water like it did you personal harm . . . Well, I mean, I guess it sort of *has* in a way . . ."

"I'm fine," Tamika said, not slowing down.

"Are you sure? Because . . . "

"I'm *fine!*"

She was being rude. One more rock on her pile of guilt, but if she stopped or focused on anything else, the memory of the nightmare would come back.

You're mean.

No.

Mean and useless.

Stop.

Pathetic.

She kept paddling, trying to put as much distance between herself and those thoughts as she could, trying to catch the enjoyment of the past two days that had been dragged away from her last night. Her paddle splashed the water and she could feel the boat going slower.

– – –

Mala pulled their kayak onto a sandbar in the middle

of the river and turned back to Tamika. "Did you eat?" she asked.

"*Yeah*," Tamika said. Mala had seen her eat the cereal bar this morning. What was she asking for?

"Anything besides that cereal bar?" Mala asked.

"Does it matter?"

"I just want to make sure you're getting everything you need. You can't paddle for hours on just a cereal bar."

"I'm fine."

"Well, how about you have a banana? And half a sandwich, too."

Tamika bit down on a groan and accepted the offer. She ate in silence. She had a harder time pushing away her thoughts while she was eating, but did feel a little better after she had finished.

Mala and Jesse seemed to be having a silent conversation through eye contact. Nothing unusual, but this time Tamika felt like it was about her.

"Tamika," Mala said, skootching closer to her. "You know, you can talk to us about how you're feeling. I know that you're going through a rough time, right now, but I'm willing to listen. We both are. If you need to talk, we're here for you."

Just like some kind of after-school special. What had she told them again? That her parents had fallen into the river or something? She looked away, not feeling up to faking an emotional breakdown, despite the real one she was having.

Maybe she could talk about the nightmare—she wanted to, in fact—but she knew that it would just make Mala feel bad. She didn't want Mala to feel bad. She was too nice for Tamika to ever want her to feel bad, but she also might feel bad if Tamika refused to talk to her about her parents, too. She was backed into a corner, no way to tell what the right answer was or even the least wrong one. Everything she did was wrong. She deserved to get caught like this. She deserved to . . .

"Ahoy, strangers!"

Tamika and the Harwells jumped at the new voice. A middle-aged white couple were floating by in a pontoon boat. They were sunburnt and smiling info-mercial-worthy smiles. Tamika had a passing thought of them trying to sell the Harwells the pontoon they were on right in the middle of the river.

And we'll be right back to your regularly scheduled mental breakdown after these messages.

Jesse's shoulders went to his ears and he looked down at his hands. Mala got to her feet and waved at the couple. Her smile seemed less genuine than usual.

"'Ahoy' to you, too!" she said.

"You folks enjoying the river?" the woman on the boat asked, her chalk-white teeth gleaming in the sun.

"Very much so, yes," Mala said. She paused. "Uhm, you know, the water's a bit shallow here. You might want to turn back."

"Oh, it'll be fine," the man said with the flippancy of a child who didn't know any better, or someone who had enough money to fix a hole in a boat.

"You sure about that?" Mala said, still trying to save them.

"Sure, I'm sure," the man said.

"We know a thing or two about pontoons," the woman said. "You know, like you know your canoes."

A flash of discomfort showed on Mala's face, but the not-so-genuine smile soon returned. "Kayaks," she said.

"Oh, right! You know, I've always wondered if that's an Indian word!" the woman said.

Tamika could see that it was getting harder and harder for Mala to keep her smile.

"I wouldn't know. I'm not Indian. Or Native American, for that matter."

"Oh! What are you then?" the woman asked, not realizing how much she was testing Mala's patience.

"A human, I'm pretty sure," Mala said.

The couple laughed. Mala laughed with them. Not her normal, joyous laugh. This one seemed as disingenuous as her smile had been.

"Well, you two have a nice day, now," Mala said. She waved them off as they drove away. As soon as they were out of sight, she dropped her hand and her smile.

"*Clueless*," she muttered to herself, then turned to her husband with a hint of concern, "Jesse?"

He nodded and gave her a thumbs-up.

"Alright," she said.

Tamika worried about Jesse. He'd practically curled in on himself when those people had shown up. She worried more that, with the distraction gone, Mala would ask her about her feelings again, but she just threw the banana peel into the woods on the other side of the river and packed the rest of the sandwich back into her bag.

"We should probably wait for them to get a little farther ahead," Mala said. "I don't want to have to make small talk with those fools all the way down the river."

Jesse said something in sign language and Mala snorted.

"What?" Tamika asked.

"He said that maybe we'll have to drag them along behind the kayaks when their boat crashes."

Tamika let out a small chuckle at that. Less worried

about Jesse, she began to imagine what kind of info-mercial that would make:

Drag-along™! The fun new craze that everyone is talking about!

"I always wanted to have a closer experience with the river. And now I can!"

Kayakers not included.

The image of the couple with their sunburnt faces and chalk-white smiles both giving a thumbs-up to the camera as a stone-faced Mala dragged them along behind her kayak made her giggle. Which soon turned into full-blown laughter.

"What's so funny?" Mala asked.

Tamika couldn't tell her. She couldn't speak over the laughter. It wasn't even that funny, but she kept laughing.

"Well, someone sure seems to be feeling better," Mala said once Tamika caught her breath without dissolving back into giggles.

She didn't know if she was feeling better or not. The laughter had left her in a lighter place, but now that it was over she could feel the dark edges creeping back in. She needed to get back to rowing.

"Yeah," she said with the biggest smile she could muster. "Let's get going."

– – –

They rowed for the rest of the day, taking small snack and sightseeing breaks. They didn't see the couple on their pontoon again, but Mala would make up "where are they now" stories about them every couple of minutes, each one more ridiculous than the last.

" . . . and she'll always tell the tale of the giant squirrel that ate her husband!"

"Wait, I thought he was her lover, last time?" Tamika said.

"Ah, that's what they *want* you to think!" Mala said.

Jesse bent over in his kayak, shaking with silent laughter.

As the sun set, Tamika started to tune in and out. She hoped that Mala would only tell silly stories at the campfire that night. Otherwise, she would have to think up some kind of excuse to go to bed early. She had rowed pretty hard that day, hardly taking any breaks. She could just say she was exhausted and it wouldn't be too much of a lie.

But they didn't stop. They had the rest of their sandwiches for dinner and then kept going. Tamika didn't complain. Focusing on rowing kept the bad thoughts at bay and left the nightmares for later, but she did wonder why they were still going. She was starting to feel tired. And spooked.

"You doin' alright, kid?" Mala asked about half an hour into rowing in the dark.

"Uh . . . y-yeah." She didn't even sound confident to herself. The darkness was getting to her, the nightmare of the River Woman coming back in full and dazzling HD. She tried to row the image away, but she couldn't go as hard as she had been. Her muscles were failing her, which just added to her creeping distress. She was shaking, though whether it was from exhaustion or fear or the cold water that kept sloshing onto her, she couldn't tell.

"Wh-when are we making camp?" she asked.

"As soon as we find a good spot," Mala said. "The forest is too thick, here. There'd be no room for a tent and it would be dangerous. Well, so is paddling in the dark, but we may have made a *tiny* miscalculation. Don't worry. It won't be long till we get to camp. Everything's going to be okay."

Tamika nodded, wondering what kind of miscalculation had put them in this situation and if it had anything to do with her. She tried to keep paddling, but was getting sloppier by the second, more like a toddler in a bath than a kayaker.

You were never a kayaker.

It was too dark. She could only see Jesse because of his reflective life jacket and neon-orange boat.

It's too dark.

"Hey," Mala said. "You want to take a little break? I mean, that's the beauty of a tandem kayak."

"N-no. I'm fine. I can do it. You-you don't have to worry about me," Tamika said.

She felt too close to the River Woman.

More like a drowning baby than a kayaker.

"Are you sure? Because it's totally okay if you need to. I'm strong enough for the both of us." Mala flexed to prove it.

Tamika tried to laugh. It came out choked.

It's too dark.

"No, no. I'm fine. It's okay. Totally fine. Wouldn't want to be a burden . . . " She was rambling. She couldn't stop herself. It was too dark. Bad things lived in the dark. Bad things that were going to pop out of the river and grab her. Talking did at least something to distract her.

She felt a pair of hands on her shoulders. She'd been dissociating so much, she had lost track of the world around her.

"Tamika," Mala said, "look at me, kid. I'm right here. You're not a burden and it's okay if you're not okay."

Tamika stopped rambling to look into Mala's eyes.

It was too dark.

She was scared.

She shouldn't be scared! If the River Woman was real, which she wasn't (*don'tthinkaboutitdon'tthinkaboutitdon'tthinkaboutit*), what was the worst thing she could do? Kill her? Hadn't that been what Tamika had come to the river for in the first place? Hadn't she lied to the Harwells to get a closer shot at it? When had she lost focus? Why was she so *scared*? Why did it feel like the darkness was closing in on her, wrapping itself around her throat? Why was her chest aching?

"Tamika," Mala said again, "just breathe. Listen to my voice and breathe. It's going to be okay. I'm here. Jesse's here. We'll be on dry land in a couple of minutes. We're not going to let anything happen to you. Take a deep breath." Mala demonstrated taking one.

Tamika copied the action. She felt ridiculous, but there was nothing else she could do. Giving all of her attention to Mala at least gave her something to hold onto.

Mala kept hold of her shoulders and talked to her, counting out her breaths or just saying encouraging words. Mala became her whole world. No bad thoughts, no dark night, no River Woman, just Mala and her words and the feel of her hands on Tamika's shoulders.

After some time—or what she assumed had been some time, as time wasn't part of the World of Mala— something interrupted Tamika's focus: the bump of the kayak against the shore. Mala helped Tamika onto dry land and wrapped her arm around Tamika's shoulders, walking her forward, still speaking in a soft, comforting voice.

Tamika took a deep breath on her own and began to reemerge back into the real world. She was exhausted, and not just physically.

Mala handed her a water bottle. "How are you feeling?" she asked.

Tamika shrugged and took a drink, forcing the water past the lump in her throat. Any words she might've spoken would have turned into tears.

"Are you okay?" Mala asked.

Tamika shrugged again. She had no idea what had come over her and she had no energy for lying. Why was she like this? A mess of a person who felt bad most of the time and couldn't decide if she wanted to be alive or dead? And why did she drag other people into it?

She could feel the lump in her throat growing. No. She didn't want to cry on top of all of this. She was so tired.

"Do you want me to stay here or do you want to be alone?" Mala asked.

Tamika just leaned into her and squeezed her eyes shut. She felt Mala's arms wrap around her. If any tears leaked out, she didn't remember them, but she fell asleep in Mala's arms.

— — —

She woke up with the sun, inside of the tent. She didn't remember moving into it, which meant that someone had carried her. How embarrassing. She was fifteen! She didn't need to be carried and she had already caused more trouble than she was worth.

At least she hadn't had any dreams or, if she had, she didn't remember them. She actually felt well rested, despite the soreness of her muscles.

Mala and Jesse weren't inside the tent, so she changed and ventured out to find them, squinting. The early morning sunlight was much brighter without the layer of tent between her and the sky. She found them by the river, sitting on the kayaks and discussing something in sign language.

Jesse noticed Tamika first and pointed her out to Mala.

"Oh! Good morning, kiddo. How are you doing?" she asked.

"I'm alright," Tamika said. "You could have woken me up. I know you like to watch the sunrise from the water."

Jesse folded his arms and shrugged, a gesture that suggested it wasn't a big deal.

"Hey, uhm . . . " Mala began, standing and rubbing her arm, "Jesse and I were talking . . . "

Oh, no.

Tamika knew that look. She knew those words and that body language: the awkwardness, the not wanting to talk about it but having to. She knew where this was going.

"You seemed pretty freaked out last night," Mala continued.

She had scared them away with that dumb thing she had done last night. They were going to send her away. Why was she like this? And why did it hurt? She hadn't even known them for that long!

"We just . . . we wanted to know if you wanted to go home?"

Wanted to go home?

"I mean, I don't want you to feel like you have to stay here, I know panic attacks suck, and I thought that maybe you wanted to go home? I mean, you can still stay if you want. That's cool, too, but you don't *have* to."

Were those . . . options? No. No, they couldn't be. There had to be something else to this.

"I'll go, if you want me to," Tamika said.

"Only if that's what you want," Mala said. "Tamika, I'd love to have you, but this is entirely your choice."

What? She had to be imagining things. No one had ever given her a choice in matters like this. Ever.

"I . . . " Every part of her brain was screaming at her to stay. People had always told her to leave and here was a couple who not only wanted her to stick around, but were allowing her to choose. On the other hand, if she stayed, the Harwells would only see her get worse. She always got worse.

But where else could she go?

"I want to stay," she said.

Mala's face lit up, any trace of awkwardness and nervousness gone.

"You do? Oh, Tamika! That's so great!" she said. "That's so brave!"

Brave?

"Not really."

Not at all.

"No, it is! It's super brave, and I'm proud of you," Mala said.

Jesse nodded vigorously.

They meant it. They were truly, genuinely proud of her. That had never happened before either and, before she had time to process anything, Mala pulled her into a hug.

With only a second's hesitation, she hugged her back.

Chapter Seven

THEY SPENT THE NEXT TWO DAYS IN RELATIVE PEACE and solitude, paddling and camping and watching Mala attempt to fish. The bad thoughts were quieter than they'd been, but Tamika was still paddling them away. And still learning to paddle, too. Mala and Jess alternated on giving her lessons, allowing her turns in the single kayak. Neither of them seemed to think that she should already know how to paddle, considering her story, which was strange, but good for her. Falling in the river was becoming less frightening, consider- ing the amount of times it had happened, and she *was* getting better. The splash-back from her paddle was growing smaller and smaller.

She hadn't had a nightmare since the one with the River Woman, but that didn't mean much. There was always a quiet spell before the nightmares picked up where they had left off. At least Mala hadn't insisted on telling any more scary stories. Tamika wondered if it was because of her. She didn't want Mala to have to give up something she enjoyed—Tamika was already slowing them down—but she was still grateful.

While Tamika was taking a turn in the single kayak, Jesse held up a hand and pointed to a part of the river that seemed to be flowing differently. Tamika squinted. *Eddies.* They looked just like they had around the rocks, except she couldn't see anything causing them and there were a lot more. This must be what Mala had been warning her about.

"Looks like we've finally come to something a little more rough," Mala said.

Tamika nodded, swallowing.

"Don't worry," Mala said. "This really isn't so bad.

In fact, it'll be good practice for the rapids coming up in . . . what would you say, Jesse? Two days?"

Jesse nodded.

"You see how the current forms itself into a little V there?" Mala continued.

Tamika looked to where Mala was pointing and, yeah, it *did* kind of look like a V. She nodded.

"The middle of that V is clear, so you just need to stay in the middle of it."

"Okay . . . "

"Watch what Jesse and I do and follow us. You're gonna be just fine." Mala turned to nod at Jesse, then pushed away.

Tamika watched their every move, trying to memorize them before she had to go. She was shaking. How was she going to navigate this while she was shaking? How was she going to navigate this when all she did was mess things up? She'd only just started to kayak in calm waters on her own.

Mala called to her from the other side, "You got this, kid! I believe in you!"

Jesse nodded and gave her a thumbs-up.

Tamika took a deep breath. She could do this. She could do this. She paddled forward, following everything that Jesse and Mala had taught her and copying every motion she'd seen them do. Her heart raced. Her entire body felt full of electricity and she couldn't tell whether it was going to shock her or power her.

And then her boat tapped Mala's.

"You did it!" Mala shouted, pulling Tamika into a somewhat awkward hug, due to the positioning. She could hear Jesse clapping.

Tamika blinked. She had. She'd really, really done it! She hadn't messed up at all!

"You said it wasn't so bad . . . " Tamika said. That had to be the only reason that she'd been able to do it: eddies were only the beginner's level.

"But you still did it! I'm so proud of you!" Mala said.

Tamika couldn't help but smile, her body still tingling with electric adrenaline. She was beginning to lose track of how many times the Harwells said they were proud of her. It was beginning to feel normal.

Chapter Eight

MALA HANDED TAMIKA HER CELL PHONE AT CAMP the next morning. Tamika blinked, too tired to wonder how it was still charged.

"It's your grandma, kid. She wants to talk to you," Mala said.

Her grandma . . . ? Bianca! Tamika took the phone.

"You have got to get this lady to stop calling me, Tami."

"Hi, Grandma! It's good to hear from you, too," Tamika said.

"Seriously. Every day. At weird times. Tell her to stop."

"Yes, I am having a great time with the Harwells."

In the past few days, Tamika had forgotten all about her alleged grandmother and the lie that had gotten her a spot on this kayaking trip. She wanted to hang up the phone and forget about it again. Every made up response to her "grandma" felt like a spit in Mala and Jesse's faces.

Wait. Had she said *every* day? What kind of battery did she *have* in this thing?

"So, Mrs. Harwell has been giving you updates?" Tamika said. She saw Mala make a face at the name Mrs. Harwell. She would have snickered if she wasn't so tense.

"Yeah, girl, didn't you know?"

"That's so thoughtful of her," Tamika said, looking Mala in the eye. The guilt gnawed at her gut, fighting for dominance with a wave of betrayal. She knew that adults talked to each other about kids, but calling her supposed "grandma" every day without telling her just didn't sit well with Tamika.

Mala smiled, which only made it worse, and Jesse

walked by to kiss Mala on the cheek as if to emphasize Tamika's comment.

"Anyway, I just wanted to let you know that you were on the missing kids list."

"Oh, is that so?" Tamika said. That could be bad, but she doubted they were looking for her here. She and the Harwells were miles from where they had started and the river was pretty far from her most recent foster home, as well.

"I know, right? Took them a whole week!" Bianca said, "Be careful, okay? I doubt they're looking too hard and it sounds like those people you're with are good people, but still. Foster kids fall through the cracks all the time."

"Right, yeah," Tamika said. She'd been counting on that little fact before all of this, but with the Harwells involved, she counted on it even more. She couldn't let them get in trouble because she had run away and lied and still didn't have the guts to off herself.

Did she even *want* to anymore?

No. No need to think about that right now. Now

the authorities were looking for her. Even if it had taken them a week, she had to be more alert to keep the Harwells in the dark.

As much as she hated it, she had no other choice.

"Love you, boo," Bianca said.

"Love you, too, Grandma," Tamika said. She hung up and handed the phone to Mala.

"Everything good?" Mala asked.

"Yeah." *No.*

"Are you sure?" Mala asked.

"She just wanted to hear my voice."

"Well, that's sweet," Mala said with a soft smile, like she was backing down from something.

Tamika wanted to ask her why she was calling her supposed grandma every day and why she hadn't told her. She supposed that Mala was just being sweet. She was a sweet person, after all, and probably figured that a grandmother would want to know how her granddaughter was doing.

Right?

Yes.

Of course.

Right . . .

– – –

Tamika remained quiet as they kayaked down the river, partially in an attempt to row the strange, conflicting emotions away and partially to keep them from spilling out of her mouth in the form of questions and confessions. They were *her* emotions and she would deal with them on her own. No one else should have to. She'd even opted for the single kayak, just to be sure.

As her muscles burned and she began to feel better, Tamika realized that she couldn't see the Harwells anymore. She had been so focused on paddling forwards that she had lost focus on what was ahead of her.

Had she passed them up? She looked back. They weren't behind her. And that was impossible, anyway.

Had she taken a wrong turn? Was that even possible on a river? Weren't they supposed to flow one way? But Mala and Jesse had all of those maps . . .

She looked all around her, but couldn't find any sign of the Harwells. She was alone.

Abandoned.

Tamika's heart rate quickened.

No! No, the Harwells wouldn't just abandon her. They weren't those kind of people. They were different! Weren't they?

She looked at the evidence: she was alone on a river she didn't know how to navigate with a few survival tools she barely knew how to use and no real idea of where she was. Somewhere in North Dakota, right? She hoped so. If she crossed the state line, things would only get worse. The Harwells were nowhere in sight and she couldn't hear Mala calling her the way she sometimes did. Had those three days after they'd given her the choice to go home been a lie? A silent sort of apology?

Sorry, but we're done with you. You're a downer and dead weight. You're annoying and you're slowing us down. Haven't you learned how useless you are to everyone yet?

Tamika had been lying to herself this whole time, hadn't she? The lessons, all the talk of pride, they were just out of pity. They were just like everyone else.

Maybe now was the time.

Tamika stared down at her distorted reflection. She could feel her already fast heartbeat speeding up. She moved a shaky hand to unbuckle her life jacket.

Before she could undo the first one though, her reflection distorted further and a different face, a physical face, took its place. Tamika screamed. It couldn't be . . . the River Woman! Her racing heart took a leap and, at the speed it was going, managed to take her whole body with it. She thrashed, though whether she was trying to get away from the face or keep herself afloat (despite the life jacket), she didn't know.

She heard a laugh. Looking over, Tamika saw a girl on her boat. Her olive-toned, lanky arms were slung over the front of the kayak and her wet, dark hair was long enough to still touch the water. She smiled at Tamika, pure sunshine and joy.

Tamika glowered back at her.

"You pushed me off," she said. She knew full well that the girl had never touched her, but she was cold and wet and annoyed and the rush of adrenaline had left her with a feeling of exhaustion and emptiness.

"Only existentially," the girl said.

Tamika narrowed her eyes. She hadn't expected an answer like that and she didn't know what to do with it.

"So, what are you doing out here?" the girl asked.

"Well, I *was* kayaking," Tamika said, struggling to doggie paddle herself back to her boat.

"Really?" The girl pushed herself off of the boat and glided over to Tamika. "'Cause you looked like you were about to jump in." She took Tamika's shoulders and spun her around in a circle. "So, I decided to join you!"

Tamika wiggled away from her, moving closer to her kayak. The girl giggled.

"I wasn't gonna jump in," Tamika muttered. Was that a lie? It might have been. She couldn't tell.

"I'm glad I persuaded you otherwise, then," the girl

said, floating on her back. Tamika wondered how she made it look so effortless. Tamika couldn't even swim. No one had bothered to teach her.

Tamika grabbed hold of the kayak and tried to pull herself back into it, which wasn't working very well. It felt like gravity, the water, *and* the kayak were all working against her.

The girl watched her. Tamika did her best not to blush or scream in frustration.

"You look like you could use some help there," the girl said.

"I'm *fine*," Tamika spat back at her. She was not fine, in many senses of the word, but she wanted to do this herself, and she did not want help from some random girl who had decided it would be fun to scare her into the water in the first place.

The girl pulled herself onto the kayak with one fluid motion.

"You don't look like you're doing fine," she said, looking down at her.

Again, Tamika didn't know how to respond, so she

just stared at the girl for a few moments. "Get off!" she finally said.

"I want to help you."

"I don't need your help!"

"It's okay to let people help you sometimes." The girl held out a hand.

Tamika paused. Why would she say something like that? If you needed help, that meant you couldn't do things on your own and if you couldn't do things on your own, you were worthless.

You're worthless.

"Shut up!" Tamika shouted at the girl because shouting at her own thoughts would be ridiculous. "What do you know! You don't even know me!"

Mala and Jesse hadn't known her when they'd decided to let her join them. Once they had gotten a glimpse, once they knew how much help she needed, they had left her, but they still didn't know her. No one in her life had ever taken the chance to really get to *know* her.

"So introduce yourself," the girl said, unfazed by

Tamika's outburst and glares. How did she manage to keep saying things Tamika didn't know how to respond to?

"I . . . I don't have to! I don't even know who *you* are!" Tamika said.

"That's part of your problem," the girl said. "If you never *let* anyone get to know you, how can you ever expect them to? And how can you expect someone to open themselves up to you if you don't return the favor?"

"Huh?" Where had *that* come from?

The girl giggled and fell backwards off of the boat.

"Come on," she said from the other side of the kayak, "I'll hold this end so you can pull yourself in."

Tamika, not knowing what else to do, followed her instruction. It took some time and it took some struggle, but she made it back in. Once she felt that the boat was stable, she muttered a "thank you" into her lap. The girl didn't respond. Tamika looked back up and around the boat, but she wasn't there.

Tamika was alone again.

And someone was calling her name in the distance. Turning around, she saw two figures in a kayak paddling towards her, the voice growing louder as they got closer.

Mala and Jesse.

Tamika waved at them, a small, awkward, shocked movement. They *hadn't* left her behind! They hadn't forgotten her!

"Tamika! Oh my gosh, kid, we were worried!" Mala said as soon as they were close enough. She pulled Tamika into a hug that nearly capsized both of their kayaks.

"I'm sorry," Tamika said, voice muffled by the fabric of Mala's shirt.

Jesse signed rapidly. His expression was difficult to read, but Tamika could tell that he was concerned.

"No, no, it's okay!" Mala said, "You took a wrong turn around Winona Island. We should have been paying more attention. I'm so sorry, honey!"

She had taken a wrong turn? Of course she had taken a wrong turn! Thinking back, she had seen little creeks branching off parts of the river all over the place. She hadn't been paying much attention to where she had been going. It had all been in her head, hadn't it?

Wait, had Mala just called her "honey"?

Jesse was signing again, more calm this time.

"Yes, I know that!" Mala said, "But she still must have been freaked out! And I know you were worried, too, I can see it!"

"What is it?" Tamika asked.

"This empties right back out into the river," Mala said. "If we hadn't come looking, we all would have met back up, anyway. But we needed to make sure you were okay."

Mala hadn't stopped hugging her and Jesse was hovering, looking her over. He pointed from her to the water with a concerned expression.

Did you fall in?

"Oh, uh, I did kind of fall in, yeah . . . " Tamika said.

Mala pulled out of the hug and held her at arm's

length so she could look Tamika over, too, her expression more worried than before.

"Are you okay? What happened?" Mala asked.

"Uh . . . " Out of the corner of her eye, she thought she saw a shadow of a girl pass through the trees on the island.

River Woman, she thought.

But that was ridiculous.

"Nothing much," she said. "I just fell and got back up. No big deal."

Mala pulled her back into the hug and stroked her hair. "Well, I'm glad you're okay," she said.

Jesse patted Tamika's back.

As they paddled to the next campsite, Tamika thought about the girl. She wondered who she was. She wondered what she had been doing in the middle of the river on her own with no floatation device. She wondered at what the girl had said to her, and if it meant anything.

Jesse had said that Mala had just made up the story

of the River Woman. There was no way that it made sense, but still Tamika wondered.

Chapter Nine

THE CAMPSITE THEY LANDED AT THAT DAY WAS more populated than Tamika was used to. People with children and RVs and tents were scattered all about the place. She felt exposed in a way she hadn't since she had joined up with the Harwells. Jesse, at least, seemed to be as uncomfortable as Tamika felt. He was fidgeting with the straps on his backpack and avoiding eye contact with everyone.

"I know it's not ideal," Mala said, "but it's private property for a few miles down and we don't have the time to go that far. It'll just be for one night."

Jesse nodded, but didn't look up or stop fidgeting with the straps.

"You two stay here," Mala said. "I'll get us a spot."

As she walked away, Tamika felt even more exposed. She shifted from one foot to the other, not knowing what else to do.

"Well, ahoy there, strangers!" said a familiar voice.

Tamika looked up to see the perfect teeth smiling inside the sunburnt face of Mr. Infomercial. Hanging on his arm was his wife/girlfriend/lover/possibly-even-sister, Mrs. Infomercial. Tamika had never learned their names and now she struggled to keep herself from laughing at the imagined memory of the couple giving the camera a thumbs-up as they were dragged along behind the Harwells' kayaks.

Jesse pulled his focus even further into the straps on his backpack.

Tamika was left to return their wave.

"Say, wasn't there a third with you?" Mrs. Infomercial asked, shielding her eyes against a sun that had already set, looking for Mala.

"She's getting us a spot," Tamika said.

Mrs. Infomercial gasped as if she had just had the most wonderful idea.

"You should get one next to us!" she said. "It'll be so much fun! We came up here to meet with our son and some of his college friends."

"Boy rented an RV all by himself as a surprise for us," Mr. Infomercial said. "He's such a good kid!"

Tamika's head hurt as she attempted to do the calculations that would result in a college student having enough money and time to rent an RV and drive it to the Middle of Nowhere, One of the Dakotas, as a surprise.

College RV™! Surprise your parents! Invite your friends!

"And you can get an eyeful of those beautiful college boys, huh?" Mrs. Infomercial winked at Tamika.

Tamika might not have parents, but she was pretty sure that that was a weird thing for a grown woman to say to a teenager she hardly knew. She let out a small, uncomfortable laugh in an attempt to humor the woman.

They stood in silence for a moment that quickly became awkward. Mr. Infomercial cleared his throat. His wife's perfect smile—she had to be his wife, right? They had a son together . . . but the birds and the bees didn't always work like that . . . But whoever she was, her perfect smile never faltered or fell. Tamika wondered if it really was just painted on.

"So, anyway!" Mr. Infomercial said. "How's the kayaking been going? Getting all buff for the missus?" He gave Jesse's arm a playful punch.

Jesse tensed and cringed away from the contact. His hands shook and he held the backpack straps in a death grip. Tamika had never seen him like this. Then again, she had only known him for a week and in all that time they had stayed away from large groups and strangers. She remembered his body language the first time they had come across the Infomercials and she knew she had to do something. Tamika was uncomfortable as well and she had no idea *what* she was going to do, but it had to be something. Jesse had done a lot for her in the past few days. It was time she stopped being such a dead weight.

She took a step forward. She wasn't shaking at all, which surprised her. Confrontation normally made her go weak in the knees, but she had never had someone else to stand up for. It filled her with a confidence that she hadn't known she had.

"Don't do that," Tamika said to the man.

Mr. Infomercial blinked and tilted his head at her. "Oh, I barely touched him!" he said with a chuckle. "I'm sure your dad is man enough to take a playful little punch, sweetheart."

Tamika narrowed her eyes, then took a quick glance back at Jesse. His eyes were focused on the straps and his shoulders were up to his ears. His brow was furrowed, though Tamika couldn't tell if it was with anger or annoyance or pure discomfort. It didn't matter. He was very clearly not okay with the contact and the comment and Tamika couldn't understand how the man could not see it.

"Back off, Mr. Infomercial," Tamika said.

The man's mouth opened, his face screwing itself into a confused stare. He didn't know what to say to her. The woman's smile looked more fake, somehow. "I'm sorry, little lady, what did you just call my husband?" she said.

Tamika balked, realizing just what she had said. That name was supposed to have stayed in her head! How had it gotten past her lips?

She felt the surge of confidence leave her. "I . . . uh . . . I-I . . . " she stuttered, back to her old self. She had been so determined to help Jesse that she had forgotten a part of what her complete uselessness entailed: she always messed everything up.

"You know, it's not nice to call people names," the woman said. She turned an expectant gaze towards Jesse. "Well? Aren't you going to reprimand your daughter?"

Both Tamika and Jesse were trapped. What were these people going to do when they realized that Jesse wasn't going to answer them? Tamika took a small step closer to him, not knowing what else to do. Where, oh where was Mala?

"What's going on here?"

Speak of the devil! Or, in this case, think of the goddess. Mala stood behind the couple, her arms folded and face stern. She wouldn't even grace these people with an ungenuine smile this time.

"Your daughter is being very rude and your husband is no help at all," the woman said, smiling a smile that was used to getting what it wanted and speaking slowly, as if she didn't expect Mala to understand her.

"Mm-hm," Mala said, "and what, *exactly*, was it that prompted Tamika—who is not my daughter, by the way—to be so rude to you?"

Tamika felt a small pinch in her chest when Mala said those words. They shouldn't bother her. Mala was only telling the truth. She *wasn't* her daughter. She wasn't anyone's daughter.

Meanwhile, Mr. and Mrs. Infomercial had the nerve to look offended.

"I don't take your meaning," Mr. Infomercial said.

"Don't you?" Mala said. "Well, I guess I'll have to speak to someone who understands words, then." She turned to Tamika and Jesse.

Jesse looked up for the first time to say something in sign language. His hands seemed to move faster than they usually did, as if all the nervous energy that was building up was trying to shoot out through the movements.

Mala's expression darkened further. She turned back to the Infomercials, who were confused at this change.

"So you were harassing my husband and bullying Tamika when she stood up for him?" Mala said in a tone Tamika had never heard her use before.

The Infomercials leaned away, shock written in bold letters on their faces. It only solidified the name Tamika had chosen for them.

"Just what are you accusing us of?" Mr. Infomercial spluttered out.

"I don't know how I can be any clearer," Mala said. "Then again, you're obviously a terrible listener." She motioned towards Jesse with one hand. "He was giving off every sign that said he didn't want to be touched and you touched him anyway." She motioned towards Tamika with her other hand. "She was telling you to back off and you refused to." She folded her arms again. "Clearly, you're too stupid for me to even be trying to make you see sense, so I think we'll take our leave of you." Mala put her arms around Jesse and Tamika and walked them away from the couple. "I'd say good day, but I really don't care if your day is good or not."

"W-we're going to report this!" Mrs. Infomercial shouted after a good long bout of shocked silence.

"Oh, go ahead!" Mala shouted back. "Cry to mommy and daddy! See where it gets you!"

She continued walking, back straight, eyes forward, not caring or listening to whatever retort the couple might have shouted back. The trio remained silent for the entire walk to their campsite where, thankfully, there was no RV in sight.

Mala reached into Jesse's backpack and pulled out

their tent gear. "Tamika, honey, could you help me set this up?" she said.

Tamika nodded, taking what was handed to her, so focused on everything that had just happened that she hardly noticed Mala calling her "honey" again.

"Thank you," Mala said as they set it up.

"For what?" Tamika asked. "I didn't really do anything. I froze up."

"But you stood up to them. You said something. I know that can be rough, especially with people who are so lost in their privileged worlds that they can't see how much they're hurting people." Mala glared into the distance, as if she knew where the couple were and was wishing ill on them.

"You don't seem to have a problem with it," Tamika muttered.

"I'm a mixed-race woman married to a nonverbal, autistic black man. I've had a lot more practice," Mala said with a shrug, turning back to continue working on the tent. "You did good, kid. You really did. I'm proud of you."

Tamika's heart did a flip. She might not be Mala's daughter, but making Mala and Jesse proud meant everything. She glanced over to where he was leaning against a tree, hugging his knees to his chest and taking slow, deep breaths, eyes closed.

"Is he gonna be okay?" Tamika asked.

"He'll be fine," Mala said. "He just needs some time to sort everything in his head back to the way it should be. It's best to just leave him to it. He knows what he's doing."

– – –

Jesse joined them for the campfire.

"Feeling better?" Mala asked him.

He shrugged and leaned his head on her shoulder.

Tamika, meanwhile, watched her marshmallow as it burned and bubbled and expanded, thinking about the events of the day: the River Girl, the Infomercials, standing up for someone for the first time in her life . . .

"I want to tell a story," Tamika said after the marshmallow had melted and the tip of her stick began to smolder. Why did she want to tell a story? She wasn't trying to fill the silence. She minded it less and less as the days passed, but a story felt right, at the moment.

Jesse lifted his head from Mala's shoulder and made a motion for Tamika to go on.

"Okay." Tamika took a breath. "Sorry if it's, you know, bad or whatever. Here goes . . .

"Once, there was this couple. A man and a woman. They were married and everyone thought they were the wisest people in the world. So the people who lived by the river asked them to help them out, because the river wouldn't listen to them and people were dying on it and stuff. The wise people went down to the river to try and figure out what they could do to help.

"When they get there, they meet this girl on the shore. She's a young girl, and she's beautiful and strange and they tell her to run along home. They say that the river is dangerous and until they sort things out she shouldn't be around.

"The girl doesn't leave. She tells them that it's fine. That the river likes her. The couple doesn't think that's possible because of all the people who said that the river isn't nice, and they tell the girl that she's just stupid and needs to listen to them because they're so wise about everything all the time. The girl just jumps into the water, then, and starts swimming around like it's the easiest thing in the world.

"The couple are shocked, but they think that the people have just been lying to them, then. That there's no way some girl could be friends with the river if the river was something that killed people. So the guy goes . . ."

Tamika deepened her voice, uncertainly trying to mimic what the man's voice might sound like.

"'That's nothing! I could do that just as easy!' And he steps into the water and the river carries him away. The woman and the man, their skin turns all white from fear, and the woman shouts for her husband, but she's at least wise enough not to follow him in.

"The girl swims up to her, then, and she says to

her, 'I can save him and bring him back to you, but it's gonna cost you.' The woman agrees and the girl dives under to go save the guy. When she comes back with the guy in her arms, she grabs the woman and drags her into the water, dunks the couple into the water, and tosses them back onto the river bank. Then the girl goes back under the water, 'cause she got what she wanted from them.

"The couple is all confused and they don't know what just happened or even why they're at the riverside, but they figure it must be for some kind of reason, so they start wandering along it. They make a bunch of mistakes along the way, but they never learn from them and they never stop because they can't find what their purpose is. 'Cause the river girl took their wisdom from them, but left their arrogance.

"So, uh, yeah. That's the story or whatever." Tamika stared into the flames of the campfire and poked the logs with her stick, mouth dry, hand shaking. She knew her story wasn't that great. She knew that she didn't have Mala's way with words or knack for horror, but she'd had to tell the story. With the kind of day she'd just had, she'd had to find some way to make sense out of it. She felt lighter after telling it, though a nervous tension had replaced her contemplative thoughts.

"Tamika, that was wonderful," Mala said.

Tamika looked up from the fire to see Jesse nodding.

"Nah," Tamika said, "I just made it up, now. It's okay. You don't have to lie, I won't be mad."

"We're not lying, though! It was good!" Mala said. "I mean, if you really want criticism, your delivery could use some work, but that comes with time and practice. What's important now is that you created something and you shared it with us. You *wanted* to share it with us! If you ask me, that's the true magic of campfire stories."

Jesse nudged Mala and said something to her in sign language.

Mala nudged him back. "*You're* corny," she said.

He was laughing his silent laugh again and Tamika

was glad to see it. She smiled back at them, the nervous tension dissipating. The last bit of the betrayal melted away with it. So what if Mala called Tamika's "grandmother" without telling her? Mala had told her, eventually, and the Harwells were so kind that it must have been a caring gesture.

She still didn't think her story was all that good, but the Harwells had liked it. It had made them happy and that was worth everything to her.

Chapter Ten

*S*HE WAS UNDER THE WATER AGAIN, JUST AS DEEP, JUST AS
dark, and just as cold as it had always been. A faint
light glimmered above her head. A neon life jacket floated
up. She tried to catch it, to be taken up with it, but she
was too late. It floated to the surface without her, making
the light ripple and shadows dance across her face. The
ripples settled as she held a hand out towards the life
jacket, knowing it was too far out of her reach. She could
see Jesse and Mala's faces. They were on the surface, above
the water. They must be so worried about her!

A warm, olive-toned hand grabbed Tamika's out-
stretched arm. The River Girl, laughter in her eyes and

long, dark hair spreading around her like a large fin. Tamika wanted her own voice to join the laughter in those eyes, but she only managed to release a few joyful bubbles to the surface. She gripped the girl's wrist, felt the warmth of that hand begin to spread through her, and the girl started to swim her upwards.

But something colder than ice latched onto Tamika's ankle before either girl could touch the surface. Tamika looked down, directly into the milky-eyed stare of the River Woman. Her skin was just as translucent, her grip just as tight. Her emaciated face had a different shape to it, though. It was hard to see, but Tamika could have sworn that she looked just like the woman from the camp. She knew that the woman's husband was waiting farther down. Just as gruesome, just as cold.

Like a prison ball chained to her ankle, the River Woman was dragging her down without moving a muscle (assuming she had muscles left to move; her hand felt as if it were all bone). The River Girl struggled to keep pulling her upwards. Tamika felt stretched. The cold from her ankle was seeping up to clash with the warmth from *her wrist. The River Girl couldn't fight her alone, but Tamika was too petrified by the woman's open-mouthed stare and the darkness below to help. One thought bubbled in her mind: she couldn't let the River Girl get dragged down with her.*

She let go of her wrist . . .

. . . and Tamika woke up gasping for breath inside the tent.

Mala was at her side.

"Tamika? Tamika it's okay, honey, just breathe. It's okay." She pulled Tamika into a hug and stroked her hair, whispering comforting things into it.

The nightmare had shaken Tamika more than most, and she couldn't reason out why. She didn't want to, either. Reasoning it out meant that she had to think about it. Instead, she clung to Mala, focusing on her voice and the feeling of her arms around her. She grounded herself in the woman, anchored herself in reality, and felt guilty for using Mala in such a selfish way.

Once she regained her metaphorical footing, Mala asked her if she wanted to talk about it.

Talking about it also meant thinking about it. She would rather pretend it had never happened, just curl up in Mala's arms and forget.

But she pulled away from Mala and turned to her backpack to start packing. "I'm fine," she said. "It was just a little nightmare. No big deal." She got them all the time.

"Okay," Mala said, not sounding convinced. She stood to leave the tent. "But I'm here if you want to talk about it," she said before she exited.

Tamika tried to focus on packing, berating herself for making Mala worry. She had used up her allowance for that back when they had been paddling in the dark.

When she finally left the tent, Mala was nowhere to be seen. Jesse, though, was sitting against a tree, eating a banana. Tamika threw him a curious look.

"Where's Mala?" she asked.

Jesse took a last bite of his banana and pointed towards the river. Mala was getting the kayaks ready.

He then jerked a thumb in the direction of the tent while looking at Tamika.

Do you want to help me take it down?

Tamika nodded and they took the tent down together, just as they had every morning for the past week. It went smoother than it had the first time, which felt like an eternity ago. Tamika knew what she was doing now and could better anticipate and interpret Jesse's movements.

As soon as they were done, Jesse put both hands on her shoulders and looked her directly in the eye. Jesse never looked anyone in the eye, aside from sometimes Mala, and he rarely touched Tamika. He was trying to tell her something that simple gestures and expressions—and maybe even words—couldn't say.

He was thanking her for the other day; Tamika felt that more than understood it. She would have denied it, but the look was so intense and the moment so special that she felt anything but acceptance would soil it.

And then it was over and he picked up some bags to

bring down to the kayaks. Tamika took whatever was left and followed.

– – –

Mala stood in the ankle-deep water, looking across the river as if observing her kingdom. "You two ready?" she asked, turning to face them.

Jesse nodded. Tamika nodded as well.

"Good!" Mala said, looking at her watch. "If we make good enough time, we can even cross the state line today!"

Tamika froze. The state line. She knew that spelled trouble, even if she didn't know exactly what kind. Cop shows talked about "crossing state lines" and caseworkers had mentioned the function of the state enough times for her to be very worried about what might happen to her or the Harwells.

Especially the Harwells.

She was on the missing persons list, after all.

You could stop them.

How?

You could stop yourself.

Could she? She hadn't been able to before. Every attempt had failed. But now the Harwells were on the line, too. She had been brave enough to stand up for Jesse. Maybe she'd be brave enough to do this, too.

– – –

Tamika paddled as hard as she could, but it didn't help anything. Her mind still roiled and, to top it all off, the image of the River Woman kept popping up just like the first time she had dreamed of her. She tried to tell herself what Jesse had told her: the River Woman wasn't real, Mala had just made her up. The Harwells would keep her safe.

As she thought on that last point, her mind dragged her back into the dream. The Harwells hadn't been there to keep her safe at all. The River Girl had been there, trying to help her, but she had only been dragged down, as well. Tamika did not want that to happen to

Mala or Jesse. Not because of her. She couldn't let it happen. She *wouldn't* let it happen.

She heard Mala from a muffled distance. She shook her head and snapped herself back to reality.

"I hate to drag you out of the Zone," Mala said, "But I think it's about time that we took a lunch break."

Had it really been that long? Tamika squinted at the sky. The sun was high, much higher than it had been the last time Tamika had noticed. She didn't feel hungry, though she probably should. She hadn't been able to stomach anything that morning, stuffing the cereal bar Mala had given her into her pocket while she wasn't looking. She felt even less hungry when she wondered if they were still in North Dakota.

Jesse was giving her a look. If Mala hadn't seen her stuff that cereal bar away, he probably had. Jesse noticed everything.

"I think we're far enough away from that campsite now to eat on shore in relative peace, don't you?" Mala said. She shielded her eyes from the sun, looking like the captain of a ship trying to steer her crew to a safe harbor.

"Yeah," Tamika said, a distant note in her voice. She turned towards the shore without waiting for Mala to start paddling.

"Hungry, are we?" Mala asked, joining her in paddling.

"Just a bit," Tamika said, forcing a smile. She still wasn't hungry, and every time her mind strayed back to the nightmare or the state line, she felt even less so, but she didn't want Mala to worry.

She had never expected to feel the kind of connection she felt with the Harwells. Maybe she'd never wanted to. Maybe she still didn't want to. She was going to have to leave them, eventually, and a deep connection would only hurt worse when it was broken.

As Mala handed her a sandwich, Tamika wondered why she hadn't realized this until now. Had she been too preoccupied with her own thoughts? Her own plan? Had her nightmares distracted her? Had the paddling? Why hadn't she processed that she was beginning to feel more than just content with them? Why hadn't her brain shut those feelings down?

Stupid.

"Tamika, honey, are you going to eat?" Mala asked.

Tamika took a bite of the sandwich she had been handed. Why had Mala started calling her "honey," anyway? Hadn't her nickname for her always been "kid" or "kiddo"? That had been fine. Why had Mala changed it?

"Are you okay, kid? You seem . . . distant."

See! "Kid." Kid was perfect. None of that intimate "honey" nonsense.

"I'm fine," Tamika said.

"If you're still worked up about that nightmare, you know you can always . . . "

"I'm *fine*," Tamika said. She wasn't fine, but that wasn't news. She had never truly been nor, she assumed, would she ever *be* fine. It was a fact that she lived with, like the fact that she was never going to meet her real parents or the fact that she was never going to be adopted. Suddenly, she remembered how much she didn't *want* to live with those facts. She felt even less hungry, the bit of sandwich she was chewing on started to feel mushy and gross in her mouth.

You came here for a reason, her mind berated her.

Things are different now, another, smaller part of her mind chimed in.

How are things different? Did you forget that you're lying to these people? That you're on the missing persons list? That the Harwells will get in trouble if you're found with them? Especially after you cross that state line?

But—

Not to mention the fact that you made those rich white people back at the camp mad. Do you really think that they're the kind of people to take that lying down? Mala made sure to say you weren't her daughter. They're going to find out who you really are and they're going to send the authorities after you. You'll be right back where you started, except innocent people will have gotten hurt in the process. That's your fault. You came here to make sure you couldn't screw up anymore and yet here you are, screwing up.

Tamika forced herself to swallow the bite of sandwich past the lump in her throat. She kept from glancing over at the Harwells and whatever cutesy thing she was sure they were doing. She had to stop this before she got any more attached, before things got any worse. She had to let go of the Harwells before she dragged them down with her.

You came here for a reason.

She had to finish what she had started. If she had a choice before, she didn't have one now. She had a duty. Anything that could help Mala and Jesse was the right thing to do, in her book.

Her stomach stopped churning and her mind paused its replay of her nightmare. She felt more focused and relaxed than she ever had. As Tamika finished her sandwich, she began to plot out the logistics: the where, when, and how. Coming to the river had been an impulse, a desperate escape attempt. It was more than that, now.

She still planned on drowning, despite her fear of the River Woman. She would swim straight into that milky-eyed corpse's arms if it came down to it. She knew she couldn't just jump into the water, though. The Harwells would notice. They would try and save her, and no amount of explaining that she was doing it for their own good would stop them. They were too good. She wished that she could just row off on her own, again, and felt an itch of annoyance at wasting her last opportunity. Mala watched her like a hawk, now, insisting that she stay in the tandem. There had to be some other way.

She looked to the river as if to ask for guidance, listening to the rushing of the water as if she could translate it into English.

Rapids.

Mala had mentioned that there would be rapids coming up while they'd been paddling, hadn't she? People died on the rapids all the time, didn't they? Especially inexperienced people. It would look like an accident. It would look like a stupid girl had run away to go on a stupid trip and had done something stupid that had ended up killing her. That was basically the story of her life, wasn't it? Bianca could back it up.

She took the last bite of her sandwich and stood, putting on her biggest, cheeriest smile like a mask.

"I'm ready to go," she said.

Mala chuckled. "Slow down, there, honey, you just ate. Do you want to vomit all over the river? Not that the fish would mind much," she said.

Tamika sat down, then paused. "I want to try the single kayak again," she said.

Mala bit her lip. "I don't know . . ."

"I'll pay more attention this time! I won't leave your sight. And I want to try the rapids for myself, anyway."

Mala turned to Jesse, who was nodding, smiling at Tamika. Encouraging her. Maybe he thought she was starting to perk up.

"Well, okay," Mala said. "I got my eye on you."

It was the most supportive use of that phrase Tamika had ever heard, but she was numb to it. Numb to everything. She just wanted to complete her plan.

They waited for half an hour, watching their

surroundings, listening to the chirps and rustles and rushing of nature. The sun was warm, but the trees they lounged under kept it from being uncomfortably so. A breeze brushed past the leaves, making the trees talk and inviting birds to glide on the updraft. The Missouri River was a nice place to die, Tamika thought. It was peaceful.

A shadow passed in the corner of her eye and she turned to look for it. It had been a familiar shape, but she couldn't place it.

"Something wrong?" Mala asked.

"No," Tamika said. It wasn't much of a lie. The shadow hardly troubled her, though it had made her curious. Either way, it didn't matter.

"You ready to get going then, eager beaver?" Mala said, "South Dakota, here we come!"

Tamika nodded, bracing herself for a rush of excitement or nervous tension.

She felt nothing.

Chapter Eleven

*I*T DIDN'T TAKE THEM TOO LONG TO COME UPON THE bout of rapids.

"Okay! You remember what I taught you, right?" Mala said.

Tamika nodded. "Stay in the V," she said. Tamika tried to paddle forwards, get it over and done with, but was stopped by Jesse's paddle. He raised a hand to his chest and inclined his head. He wanted her to watch them first. Tamika allowed this. It would be easier if they were already ahead of her, anyway. The current, on its own, was hard to fight, but rapids were harder still.

They went ahead as Tamika watched. Her kayak was sandwiched between the current and a rock, keeping her from following the Harwells before she was ready. Mala whooped as she and her husband navigated the white water like champions. They shifted their weight together, paddled, and weaved in perfect sync. Tamika had never seen Jesse move so fluidly. The rush of the water must have inspired his blood to rush along with it. They were having such a great time that it almost hurt Tamika to think about what was about to happen.

But it didn't hurt. The feeling of guilt, like most of her other emotions, had dulled until it was almost nothing. Everything she had was focused on one thing and one thing only: taking herself out of the picture so the Harwells wouldn't suffer.

"You ready, kid?" Mala shouted over the roar of the rapids.

Tamika snapped her attention to her. Her eyes had lost focus at some point during their display, but now they took in Mala, in vivid detail. Every frizz and stray curl of her eternally messy hair, the warm brown of her skin, the earnest gleam of her sea-green eyes, the genuine smile that lit her face all burned themselves into Tamika's mind.

I'm doing this for you, she thought. *You're the best thing that's ever happened to me in my whole life and I'll only ever drag you down otherwise.*

Some part of her wanted to say something, an apology for existing and for ceasing to exist. She wanted to tell them how much the short time she had spent with them had meant to her. She wanted to tell them that what was about to happen wasn't their fault, that she was content with her decision.

But she couldn't say any of that. She didn't have the words and she didn't have the time and she couldn't take the risk, so she just nodded.

"I'm ready."

She pushed away from the rock, dropped her paddle, and unbuckled her life jacket.

The world around her dulled. The rushing water sounded like it was miles away. Her hands were steady.

The buckles unclipped easily. She shrugged the jacket into the water, a bright splash of neon floating away with nothing to hinder or pull it down.

She didn't even have to rock the boat. Without anyone steering it, it crashed into a few rocks, was over-balanced by a dip in the path, and tossed Tamika into the water all on its own.

She heard Mala's scream before she went under.

The current tossed her from side to side, tearing her in several directions at once. She kept her body limp, hit a few rocks, and in all the rushing and confusion and pain, a thought surfaced.

I don't want to die.

It was as if a switch had flipped in her brain. She didn't. She didn't want to die. She truly, genuinely, did *not*. Her body began to thrash, trying to get above the water.

I don't want to die. I don't want to die.

She had no idea which way the surface was. She didn't know what was up or down or sideways.

I don't want to die. I don't want to die!

Her lungs burned. Darkness crept into the edges of her vision.

I don't want to die!

It was too late. She had realized too late.

Idon'twanttodie!

She slammed into something solid and lumpy and painful, knocking whatever air she had left out of her. The darkness closed in.

Chapter Twelve

*D*ARKNESS.

Darkness and coldness and nothingness.

That was all. That was the only thing that was, if it was anything at all. If it had any ability to be.

Stupid girl.

She was falling.

No, she was floating. Floating downwards, lighter than anything, towards the cold, dark nothingness.

Where are you going?

She couldn't move or think to accept or reject anything. She was just floating. She was going nowhere, doing nothing, indefinitely.

Come back.

Back? Had she come from somewhere? Was she leaving someplace? Was she someone? She couldn't remember. Everything was nothing. Maybe the faint, dull, fuzzy glow of something—a memory, perhaps—was somewhere, but if she was leaving somewhere then it was leaving, as well, and it was going in a different direction.

Come back.

What was that voice? It wasn't her voice. Or was it? Did she have a voice? So many things she didn't know. So many things, it was beginning to trouble her, but how could she be troubled over nothing?

Come back, stupid girl!

Light and blurry colors erupted into her vision. The nothingness was gone, replaced by everything. Overwhelming. She couldn't make sense of it. Her thoughts and memories were still trapped in the nothing she had emerged from.

She heard the voice that had called her back to everything say, "Breathe."

Her body followed the instruction on instinct, then

spasmed, jerking her thoughts and memories back into their rightful place. She was back. Every part of her was back where it belonged—and it was awful.

She coughed and hacked, her lungs refusing to let her catch a decent breath. Her entire body ached. She was sure that something was broken, or at least deeply bruised. Her eyes and nose and throat burned and she shivered, still coughing, still trying to breathe.

Something turned her onto her side. The coughing stopped, eventually, even if none of the other pain did.

When she was able to focus on something other than getting air into her lungs, she wondered what had happened. Where was she? How had she gotten here? Why was she here?

"Are you done, yet?"

And whose was that voice that had dragged her out of the abyss?

She attempted to catch a glimpse of the person and every muscle in her body protested. She groaned instead. Lucky for her, the person leaned over to look her in the eye. Long, dark hair draped over her shoulder and splayed across the grass. She recognized the olive-toned face, but not the annoyed expression on it.

"I said are you done?" the River Girl repeated.

"Am I dead?" Tamika managed to croak after staring at her in silence for a few moments.

The girl rolled her eyes. "No, you're not dead," she said. "I just saved your life, you stupid girl." She hopped over Tamika and collapsed on the ground next to her, annoyed expression turned up to the sky. "And I'm not so ethereal and mysterious that you should think you were dead when you see me."

Once again, Tamika had no idea how to respond to anything this girl said, so she just continued to lie on her side and stare at her. She could have sworn that the girl had been more smiley the last time she'd seen her, but she could also be wrong. It was hard to even keep her in focus. Her head throbbed. She must have hit it on something as she was dragged along by the current. She must have hit everything on something. There was not a single part of her body that wasn't experiencing some kind of pain.

As the girl wasn't forthcoming with any kind of conversation and Tamika couldn't find it in her to think of something to say or force her sore throat to say it, she began to reflect on what had just happened.

She had attempted suicide.

She had avoided the word for so long and even now she winced when she thought it—or had she just disturbed another forming bruise? It had sounded over-dramatic, something on TV that was always blown out of proportion to a point that she simply could not connect it to anything she was feeling. But now, after the rapids had beaten her half to death and she had managed to come out alive, she had to deal with the facts. She had tried to kill herself.

But she was still alive.

That fact filled her with so much relief and so much shame that she didn't know which emotion was stronger. Tears burned her eyes. It hurt to sob, but her body gave her no other choice. The emotional pain might have started the tears flowing, but the physical pain kept them coming. Everything hurt. *Everything.*

The River Girl finally turned back to her. Tamika's vision was too blurred by tears to properly see her expression, but she figured that it was the same as before. The girl scooted closer and pulled Tamika into her arms, which made her sob harder. The hug hurt because everything hurt, but she didn't want her to let go. The girl's arms felt like a safe place to be, arms that had saved her life. She sobbed even harder, practically wailing. It was the only thing that could relieve some tiny fraction of the pain she was feeling. She couldn't even hug back or catch her breath enough to thank her.

"Hey, come on, now. That's enough of all that," the girl said, her tone gentler. She held Tamika and continued to mutter words and sounds of comfort until the wracking sobs turned into small hiccups.

"We finished with the dramatics, now?" the girl asked.

"Why did you . . . why did you save me?" Tamika asked. The girl sighed.

"I'll take that as a 'no,'" she said. She pulled away from the hug, but kept a hold of Tamika's shoulders so she wouldn't fall over.

"I saved you because you needed to be saved. I mean, I wasn't just going to let you drown because you thought your life wasn't worth living."

Tamika found herself staring at the girl again. How had she known her intentions? In fact, how had she even found her? It had been a full day and many miles since they'd met, and Tamika couldn't remember her having any kind of watercraft.

"I could see it in your eyes," the girl said. "When we met and you were looking into the water, I could see your soul crying—don't look at me like that. We both know that that's what it feels like."

It sounded silly but, thinking about it, Tamika had to agree. It *had* felt like her soul had been crying. It still did, in a way, but Tamika was tired of her own tears.

"So I got in my mom's boat and I followed you. I've lived on this river my whole life. I know how to follow someone without them noticing."

Oh. Well, that sounded more simple and down-to-earth than what she'd been thinking. Maybe even a little creepy. Still, the girl had saved her life. She couldn't care too much about the methods.

"Look," the girl continued, "I know that you might think that the world would be better off without you or that dying is the only way to make the pain stop, but that's not true. Don't let your brain make you think that it is and don't let your soul lead you off a metaphorical cliff."

Why should I? I don't even know you.

She knew Tamika well enough. She somehow understood the kind of pain Tamika was in. She had saved her life.

Why should I? What if you're wrong?

"Please." The girl sounded desperate. "I've been to that cliff. It's not any better."

She had? But she was so bright and wonderful and beautiful and brave. She was nothing like Tamika. But maybe . . . maybe she was a better liar.

"How?" Tamika finally decided on. She felt more

sobs bubbling in the back of her throat. She was so tired.

"By remembering the last thing you thought when you knew you were going to die," the girl said.

Tamika remembered.

"Tell me. Say the words."

"I don't want to die," Tamika said.

The girl nodded. "Hold onto that," she said. "Hold onto it for just a minute. Just an hour, a day, remember that you don't want to die. Because it doesn't last, Tamika. These feelings? They go away."

Tamika thought about it. She wasn't sure how much she believed, but this girl, this stranger, wanted to help her. She cared enough to follow her all the way into the rapids to make sure she stayed alive. And if she knew this feeling . . .

"Okay," Tamika said.

The girl pulled her into another hug, satisfied.

"I'm going to leave you my number," she whispered. "I want you to call me. When you need to talk.

When you feel bad. When you feel like you can't keep going, I want you to call me."

Tamika found that she had raised her aching arms to wrap around the girl's torso. She felt safe with her, like nothing could hurt her.

"C-can I call you for other stuff?" Tamika asked. She didn't want to lose that feeling of safety.

"You can call me whenever you want to for whatever reason," the girl said, "but those other times, you *have* to call me, or at least someone you can talk to. Trust me. I know what you're going through. I know."

She kissed Tamika on the cheek, laid her back down on her side, scratched something in the dirt, and was gone. Tamika wondered where she was going. She wondered where she had come from. Was she some kind of guardian angel? *Was* she the River Woman? Or the River Girl? She had said she wasn't some mysterious entity, but the way she had saved Tamika, the way she made her feel, there was no way that girl was anything less than divine.

And now Tamika was alone again with her thoughts

and what she assumed was a number scratched into the dirt.

"Tamika!" a panicked voice shouted.

She wouldn't be alone for long.

Chapter Thirteen

MALA AND JESSE ENCIRCLED HER IN A HUG, CLUNG TO her as if she could fade away at any second. Mala was crying. Jesse was shaking.

"We thought you were dead!" Mala gasped through sobs. "We thought we weren't going to find you! We thought you were dead!" She pulled away to kiss every part of Tamika's face before pulling her back into the hug.

"Oh my God," she muttered into Tamika's shoulder, "Oh my God oh my God oh my God."

After a very long period where the Harwells just held her, making sure she was really there, Mala asked the question that Tamika had been dreading to answer: "What happened?"

Tamika looked into Mala's eyes. She could see a mix of frantic worry and utter relief there. She turned to look into Jesse's. His held the same emotions, though not as readily visible. Tamika looked down and began to cry again. She really didn't want to, but with the way the Harwells were acting, on top of everything else, she couldn't help herself. The guilt was returning. She had upset them so much. They were far too kind to deserve that.

They pulled her back into the hug, Jesse rocking them all until Tamika was able to form words again.

"I'm sorry," she said, "I'm so sorry."

Mala shook her head into Tamika's shoulder. "No, no. Honey, this is our fault," she said. "You weren't ready. We should have just walked around or—"

"No," Tamika cut her off, "no, it wasn't your fault. It was mine."

"Tamika, honey, no—" Mala was probably going to

say something comforting, something to ease Tamika's conscience. She still didn't understand.

"It was," Tamika said. She needed to set the record straight once and for all. "I didn't fall in. I jumped."

Jesse and Mala pulled away, still holding her, and gave her identical confused and concerned looks.

"I-I took off my life jacket," Tamika continued, her voice growing shaky, "and I jumped in." She looked down. She couldn't say any more. Her whole body shook. She had no idea how they would react. And this wasn't even half of it! She had lied, she had used them the entire time she had known them to get to this point.

You . . .

NO! She shoved the voice as far away as she could. She had made a promise. She wasn't going to let that be a lie, too.

Mala wasn't saying anything. Tamika risked a look up. She caught Jesse's eye, figuring it would be a safer place for her gaze to land. The question there was apparent: *Why?*

"I-I just . . . " Tamika felt like crying again and yet she didn't feel like crying. She was still soaking wet, but she felt dried out.

"I didn't want to be alive anymore." It all began to spill from her, like the only liquid that was left in her body. "My life sucks. I don't live with my grandma. I don't have a grandma. I don't have parents. I never had parents. I'm a foster kid. A dumb, stupid foster kid who's always messing everything up. I can't keep friends, I can't keep foster families, and I can't keep myself from screwing up everyone's lives. Including mine! I lied to you guys. I came to the river to kill myself and I couldn't even get that right. I used you guys to get closer to the water and, I don't know, it sounds stupid when I say it, but I just didn't want to keep messing everyone's lives up and hurting people and lying to people and—" She ran out of things to say. She couldn't even finish her thoughts up nicely. They just stopped.

The Harwells pulled her into a tighter hug.

"It's okay," Mala was saying. "It's okay. It's all okay."

"No, it's not," Tamika said past the lump in her throat, feeling like she would never be able to get rid of it. She was exhausted in every way imaginable. She wouldn't be sitting up if not for the Harwells keeping hold of her.

She began to lose track of time and meaning. Motions and feelings blurred together and the next time she could think clearly she was lying in Mala's lap and staring at a campfire while Mala stroked her hair. Jesse was sitting next to them, watching the fire and poking it with a stick, glancing back at Tamika every so often. When he caught her gaze, he nudged Mala and nodded at Tamika

"Are you back with us, honey?" Mala asked.

"Don't call me that," Tamika muttered. After everything she had put them through, after all the lies, she didn't deserve to be called "honey" by anyone.

"Okay. I'm sorry." And *still* Mala was the one apologizing. Tamika would never understand the woman.

"Everything hurts," Tamika said after a long pause.

"Well, the rapids aren't really a good place to go swimming," Mala said, an attempt to inject some kind of humor into the situation. It fell onto flat silence. "We're going to take you to a doctor, once the car gets here," Mala said.

Car? What car? The Harwells didn't have a car . . . Oh, right. Their friend was following them with one.

"Our friend was a little behind us, so it might take them a while," Mala continued, "but as soon as they're here, we're going to get you some proper medical care."

And get Tamika off their hands. She tried to tell herself that she was okay with this, that it was going to happen anyway, but she still didn't want to go back to the life she had been leading before. She wanted to stay with the Harwells more than anything. It was impossible, but that didn't stop her from trying to at least extend the trip.

"N-no, it's fine," she said, "I can still . . . " But she couldn't even move. She couldn't even finish the sentence. She felt another bout of tears coming on and hated herself for it.

Mala was still stroking her hair. She tried to focus on that.

"Shhhh," Mala said. "It's alright. We don't have to think about it all right now. How about we tell a story instead? It's not a real campfire without a story."

Tamika thought about that. A story sounded nice and a story from Mala sounded wonderful. She wanted to just listen and fall asleep and forget, but she knew that her mind would never let her.

She had to tell *her* story, now.

"I want to tell it," Tamika said, "I want to tell the story."

She could feel Mala smiling down on her.

"Okay. Whatever you want, hon . . . Tamika."

"It's a true story," Tamika said. "It's my story."

She felt Mala shift and she saw Jesse straighten. She hadn't told her story very well the first time. She had been so stressed and overwhelmed that it had all come out in a jumble of confession. She was going to think it through this time. Choose her words carefully. Maybe, with a story, everything that had happened would be easier to process.

"My parents, the biological ones, left me at the hospital. Or maybe it was just my mother. I don't really know. There aren't any clear records of them. I didn't look very hard. Neither of them ever came back, and I've still never met them. I used to think that maybe I could find them, do a sort of Annie thing, but I gave up on that a long time ago. It wasn't realistic and things now aren't anything like they were back in her day. She wasn't even real, just a character in a play.

"I bounced around from foster home to foster home after that. Some people were nice, some were not so nice. Sometimes homes were crowded and uncomfortable, and sometimes it was just me and it was still uncomfortable, but I never got to stay anywhere for too long. After a while, I kind of figured it had something to do with me. Other kids got to stay at places longer. Other kids were even adopted by their foster families, but not me. No matter how hard I tried.

"I never had that many friends. I didn't stay in any place long enough to get any, and people always just looked at me like I was some kind of charity case or something to be pitied when they found out that I was a foster kid, anyway. I just . . . I don't know . . . it felt like they couldn't really see me. I mean, if they could, they probably wouldn't like what they saw, anyway, so I guess it really doesn't matter all that much."

"There was no one?" Mala asked, concerned. She hadn't stopped stroking Tamika's hair and Tamika was grateful for that.

"Not really. I mean, there's Bianca, but we never get to see each other and it's hard to keep in contact." Tamika paused, trying to figure out how to confess the next part. "Uhm . . . you, uh, you know her as my 'grandmother.'"

"Yeah, I had a feeling that wasn't your real grand-mother," Mala said.

Tamika paused. "What?"

"She *did* sound like a bit of a caricature," Mala said.

"And the rest of your story . . . well, I've heard a lot of kids lie to me over the years. I've learned how to tell."

"You . . . you knew I was lying?" And they had still let her come along, had still been so nice to her?

"Yeah."

"You could've . . . called the police or something . . . " Tamika had no idea how to take this.

"And, considering all that's happened, maybe I should have . . . "

Tamika flinched, feeling guilty all over again.

" . . . Or maybe it wouldn't have changed anything. Maybe it would have made things worse. I don't know. I just know that you seemed to be having a rough time and I thought that maybe this was the best way to help. Sometimes . . . the system doesn't do things right. I guess I just didn't trust it enough to send you off to it without making sure."

Tamika felt like crying again. "You . . . You could've . . . gotten in trouble . . . *a lot* of trouble."

"I know. And sometimes that's worth it. And

sometimes it's wrong, but it was the choice Jesse and I made, and we don't regret the time we've had with you."

Tamika went silent for a while, fighting back the tears. Had she really been worth it? This whole time?

Jesse made a motion for her to continue her story.

"Uhm . . . I, uh, I guess you figured out that I ran away, then. It really wasn't hard. The foster family that I was with didn't pay a lot of attention to me. Bianca only found me on the missing persons list the other day."

Jesse shook his head disdainfully. Was he disappointed that she had run away or disappointed in the system that had taken so long to notice her disappearance? She wasn't sure anymore.

"I . . . I hitchhiked up here. I figured the river would be a good place to disappear. People . . . people drown all the time and, like, I figured it would be pretty or peaceful or whatever."

That had not been her experience in the rapids. It had been more like a rush of every anxiety conceivable.

Peaceful was the last thing she had felt. Mala wrapped her arms around Tamika and held her. It took a few minutes for Tamika to find her voice again, the tears even more threatening.

"I couldn't do it. I tried to run into the water and jump off of things, but for some reason I couldn't do it. I was still trying when I met you guys. I-I didn't want anyone to know what I was doing a-and I thought . . . I thought that . . . that *m-maybe*, if I was closer to the water . . ."

She couldn't finish the sentence, but going by the look on Jesse's face, the Harwells understood what she was getting at.

"Shh, it's okay," Mala whispered.

But it wasn't okay. She had to finish. "I-I lied to you," she said.

"I know," Mala said. "It's okay."

"N-no! It's not. It's . . . I-it's . . . I didn't lie because I had to, I . . . wanted to *use* you and I invaded on your fun and I was just . . . that was just proof to me . . . th-that I needed to get-get rid of myself."

The tears came, but she spoke through them. "B-but you're so *nice* and I was actually . . . I was actually *enjoying* myself and-and-and I kept p-putting it off until . . . until I *knew* that I was gonna cause you trouble because . . . b-because there were gonna be *police* and questions and I didn't want to go back, so I—" She choked on a few sobs. Mala held her close, her tight, comforting arms wrapped around Tamika's bruised body, and rocked her.

"I figured that rapids would work," Tamika said once she caught a breath that didn't hitch on a sob. "It would look like an accident. I wouldn't be dragging you down with me. You'd be free." Tamika took a moment to think about that. "B-but that's stupid, isn't it?" she said, angry with herself, "That d-doesn't make sense. You were still with me, a runaway, and the cops wouldn't know that it was an accident or whatever, and *then* you probably would have blamed yourselves or something 'cause you're too good. What is *wrong* with me?" She muttered the last sentence and curled into herself.

Mala and Jesse were silent and still for a moment.

"Tamika," Mala said, pressing her face against Tamika's, "there is *nothing* wrong with you."

Chapter Fourteen

*S*WIRLING COLORS SURROUNDED HER: BLUES AND GREENS *and whites and blacks. It was a rush. Nothing was set, everything was in flux, and none of it was comprehensible. She let it rush by her, knowing that it wasn't within her power to stop it, to even try.*

Where was she? What was happening? These questions and their answers rushed away as soon as they had come.

She was calm. There was an odd sense of peacefulness that came with the acceptance that things were out of her hands.

The pale, emaciated face of the River Woman rushed

past. She tried to grab at Tamika with her bony hands, but couldn't get a solid grip before she was dragged away. The River Girl was thrown past after her, her long dark hair trailing behind her. The faces of Mala and Jesse appeared out of the rush, but they didn't fly past the way the others did. They didn't stop, but circled around Tamika, their features and expressions blurring.

This unsettled her more than anything else. She wished they would stop and solidify or move along as the others had, but they continued to circle her.

Around and around and around and . . .

– – –

Trees rushed past the backseat window. The road was bumpy and uneven and it aggravated Tamika's sore body. In retaliation, it had woken her up. Among the aches and pains she was experiencing, she felt a gentle hand on her arm. Her head was in Mala's lap, again. Mala was looking out the window, contemplative, and had not yet noticed that Tamika was awake. Her hand was still. Tamika shifted some, but Mala did not turn to look at her.

She saw the back of Jesse's head and shoulder peeking out from the passenger's seat. Their friend was driving. Tamika hardly remembered getting into the car.

Tamika caught Jesse's eye in the rearview mirror before he turned his gaze back to the road. He didn't try to alert Mala or do anything to acknowledge that she was awake.

Tamika felt something shift in her stomach that didn't have anything to do with her injuries or car-sickness, something that knew she would never see the Harwells again. They would drop her off at the nearest authority, answer whatever questions needed to be answered, and be on their way. Tamika would go back into foster care. She would go right back to the miserable life she had led. She knew she was too much of a hassle to have around, despite what Mala had said.

She tried to hold onto what the River Girl had told her.

I don't want to die.

But she sure didn't want to keep living the way that she had. There was no other escape. Tamika wanted to call the girl or text her and ask her what she should do. She'd asked Mala to write down her number before they'd left, but Mala hadn't been able to find it. Maybe she and Jesse had trampled over it in their rush to get to Tamika, maybe it had never been there at all. Either way, Tamika still didn't have a phone and she didn't want to ask to use Mala's. The woman felt distant from her. If Jesse didn't want to disturb her, then Tamika was sure not going to.

She kept as still as she could, her head in Mala's lap, thinking and dreading and in pain. She didn't know where they were going or how long it would take them to get there, but she felt that her future was already set in stone. No matter how many times she thought about how she didn't want to die, the bad thoughts crept into the corners of her mind and pressed on her.

She didn't know how much time had passed before

they drove up to a hospital parking lot. Mala moved slowly, as if trying not to wake Tamika.

"I'm awake," Tamika said.

"Oh," Mala said. She rubbed Tamika's arm. "Do you think you can walk?"

"Don't know," Tamika said. She didn't feel up for trying, anyway. She wasn't willing to just walk back into her old life.

"Is it okay if I carry you?" Mala asked. Tamika nodded. She'd run out of words.

She was tired.

Mala scooped her up and carried her towards the hospital.

For a half second Tamika considered dropping from her arms and running, sprinting away from whatever fate had in store for her. In the half second after she had formed this thought, her body reminded her that it wasn't going to be able to do that.

Instead she pulled her mind away, entirely. The pain dulled. She didn't notice the Harwells admitting her to the hospital, she hardly felt the time they spent in the waiting room, and the transfer to a room with a doctor and nurses was all a blur.

"Yes, it hurts."

"Yes, I can feel that."

"No, I can't move that."

"I fell into the rapids."

Sometime later she was sitting in a hospital bed, a cast on one of her arms, bandages in various other locations, and pain medicine in her system, which at least helped her to disconnect.

The appearance of two women, one of whom was very familiar, snapped her out of her comfortable numbness. Nervous tension crept back in and clenched its iron grip on her stomach.

Evette Rowland had walked into the room with a police officer in uniform. Evette—and she had insisted that Tamika call her Evette very early on—was the social worker in charge of Tamika's case. She was a friendly woman, always ready with a smile that had never seemed genuine. Her smile was too big, too permanent a fixture on her pale, white face. Tamika had learned, over the years, that half of the time the woman only pretended to listen and proceeded to talk down to Tamika later as if Tamika would never be able to understand her own feelings and her own situation. She was frustrating, to say the least, and depressing to be around, to say the worst.

"Hello, Tamika!" Evette said, smile plastered onto her face. "How are you feeling?"

Tamika didn't answer. She *felt* that the answer to that question should be obvious.

Evette plowed right along. "This is Officer Braedon," she said, gesturing to the woman in uniform. "She wants to ask you some questions about your little *incident*." She leaned forward a bit as she said it, scrunching up her smile as if Tamika had wet the bed, not run away and nearly drowned.

Officer Braedon gave Evette an odd look. Tamika thanked whatever powers that be that someone in this room had some sense.

"This is all confidential," Officer Braedon said, still giving Evette that look. Evette didn't seem to understand that she was being dismissed. She sat down, smoothing out her skirt and taking out her ever-present clipboard. The officer closed her eyes and sighed. "Ma'am, if you would please." She gestured to the door.

"Oh . . . " Evette said. "Uhm . . . " She put her clipboard away, awkward and unsure. "Right. Yes, of course." Evette stood up and walked to the doorway, pausing as if she expected to be invited to join them. When she was not, she let out a subtle huff and closed the door behind her.

"Okay." The officer pulled the chair Evette had vacated up next to Tamika's hospital bed. She sat down and smiled a gentle smile. Tamika didn't trust police as a general rule, but this one had just kicked Evette out of the room. That was good enough for her.

"It's Tamika, right?"

Tamika nodded.

"Do you think you could tell me about what happened?"

The officer left the blank wide open for Tamika to

fill in—and fill it in she did. The story poured out of her mouth just as it had with the Harwells, only this time she was out of tears to cry. She had her thoughts a little more together, though. Officer Braedon nodded to assure Tamika that she was listening. She didn't write anything down, though Tamika was sure she would remember it in detail. Officer Braedon asked a few questions to clarify some points, but mostly she was silent, listening.

Tamika told her about running away. She told her about how she had planned to kill herself. She told her about the Harwells and what wonderful people they were. She told her that they hadn't known she was a runaway, that they had thought they'd had permission to take her along, even though she now knew that wasn't true. She told her how good they had been to her, how they had tried to help and never blamed her for lying to them. She begged the officer to let them off the hook. She begged her to make sure that the Harwells didn't get in trouble. She begged and she begged and she ended the story with begging, but she didn't feel pathetic. If she could do *anything* to help those wonderful, kind people to whom she had done so much wrong, she would. Not much else mattered to her, now. One little thing to live for.

Officer Braedon held up a hand to stop her. "I'm not going to arrest them," she said. "No one is. They've already been spoken to and, with all that you've been saying, it's pretty obvious that they had nothing to do with you running away or getting hurt."

Tamika let out a breath.

"Do you want to speak with them?" Officer Braedon asked.

Tamika looked down. She wasn't sure. Speaking with them meant saying goodbye, but not speaking with them meant that she would never see them again. She didn't want all of this to end, but she knew it was coming and she figured that she might as well end it, herself, rather than let the universe end it for her.

"Yeah," Tamika said, looking up at the officer. "Yeah, I wanna talk to them." She looked back down. "Please."

Officer Braedon nodded and left the room. A few moments later, the Harwells walked in. Tamika could hear Evette's annoying voice just outside the door, making "polite suggestions" that might end up with her being let into the room, as well. Tamika was glad when the door closed behind the Harwells without Evette's foot getting in the way of it.

"Hey, kid," Mala said, sitting next to her. Her smile held some kind of nervousness in it. Her hand rested near Tamika's, as if some invisible barrier was stopping her from touching it. "Doing any better?"

Tamika shrugged.

"Yeah, I figured that," Mala said. She looked back to Jesse and the couple shared a silent conversation that Tamika couldn't understand. She felt awkward and left out, but that didn't matter. Tamika had asked for them to be sent in for a reason and she was going to follow through with it.

"I wanted to say goodbye," Tamika said, suddenly and a little louder than she had meant to. "A-and thank you," she continued in a quieter tone, "for e-everything. For listening. A-and letting me come along with you. And I'm sorry about all the stuff that happened and for slowing you down and stuff. B-but it was really great until all that bad stuff! And I had a good time and . . . yeah. Thanks." She paused. "So . . . bye, then." Tamika looked down, not wanting to see what their expressions were, and waited for them to leave.

"Hey, Tamika," Mala said.

Why hadn't they left yet?

"If . . . if you could stay with us, would you want to?" Mala said.

Tamika looked up, eyes narrowed in confusion. "But I can't stay with you," she said, "I have to go back into foster care now." She didn't understand the point in considering impossible hypotheticals.

"But if you could, though," Mala said, "I mean, it's okay if you say no. It really is. It's been a rough couple of days."

Jesse nodded, his intense eyes emphasizing Mala's point.

Tamika thought about it, allowed herself to imagine what it would be like. Staying with the Harwells, with no lies or secrets between them, would be like a rare, wonderful dream. Then she stopped herself from thinking about it, not wanting whatever hope she might still have to be crushed by reality.

"Yeah," Tamika said, resigned. "Yeah, I'd love to stay with you." She refused to lie to the Harwells anymore. She had done more than enough of that.

The nervous hint in Mala's smile vanished. It became full and beautiful and excited. "Well, Jesse and I feel the same," she said.

Jesse nodded again, more vigorously.

Tamika narrowed her eyes in confusion again. What could possibly make them want to stay with her, after all that she had put them through?

Mala moved her hand to cover Tamika's.

"We want you to stay with us, Tamika," she said. "We just . . . it's hard to explain, but Jesse and I discussed it after you told us everything and, I don't know, we feel like you just belong with us." She wove her fingers into the spaces between Tamika's. "We click."

Tamika stared at Mala, not saying anything. She couldn't be suggesting what she thought she was. It was impossible. It was something that she didn't even dare to think about because it was so impossible.

Jesse leaned forward to touch Tamika's shoulder, and she turned to him. The look he gave her told her that it *was* possible.

"You want . . . you want to . . . ?" Tamika couldn't bring herself to say the word, but she felt happier than she had in a long time.

"Yeah," Mala said.

Tamika's face broke into a smile. The biggest, most genuine smile she had ever smiled. The Harwells hugged her and she hugged them back with as much might as her bruised body was capable of.

"It won't be easy," Mala said, "but neither is kayaking down the Missouri." She kissed the top of Tamika's head. "And when we're done with this, we're gonna finish that trip. As a family."

Tamika nodded. For the first time in her life, she felt loved.